"Admit it. Admit you want me."

She tipped back her head, desperate to deny his words.

"Admit it," Leo grated. "You have from the very first time we met."

"I'm...not going to marry you," Maddy asserted raggedly. "I'm not going to be used just for your convenience."

"You won't have much choice.... And, believe me, I shall expect to get my money's worth," he added, letting his gaze slide slowly down over her in an insolently detailed appraisal, lingering over every curve. "Every last penny's worth."

SUSANNE McCARTHY grew up in south London, England, but she always wanted to live in the country, and shortly after her marriage she moved to Shropshire with her husband. They live in a house on a hill with lots of dogs and cats. She loves to travel—but she loves to come home. As well as her writing, she still enjoys her career as a teacher in adult education, though she works only part-time now.

Books by Susanne McCarthy

HARLEQUIN PRESENTS
1717—SATAN'S CONTRACT
1748—A CANDLE FOR THE DEVIL

SUSANNE McCARTHY

Forsaking All Others

Harlequin Books

TORONTO • NEW YORK • LONDON
AMSTERDAM • PARIS • SYDNEY • HAMBURG
STOCKHOLM • ATHENS • TOKYO • MILAN
MADRID • WARSAW • BUDAPEST • AUCKLAND

ISBN 0-373-11850-3

FORSAKING ALL OTHERS

First North American Publication 1996.

Copyright © 1996 by Susanne McCarthy.

Printed in U.S.A.

CHAPTER ONE

"THAT was Uncle Leo's car!" Jamie glanced up from the hand-held computer game that was his latest obsession, his brown eyes alight with excitement as a sleek silver-grey Aston Martin appeared behind them on the quiet road that led from the suburbs of Stockport towards the contrasting wildness of the Peak District and overtook the elderly Escort Estate in one smooth manoeuvre. "Isn't it super? It does almost two hundred miles an hour."

"Does it really?" Maddy responded drily. "Pity the speed limit's only seventy."

"Oh, Uncle Leo never goes too fast," her son confided. "Though he can when he's in Germany—they don't have a speed limit there, and I bet he really bombs along!"

"I expect he does," Maddy conceded. "Remind me never to accept an invitation from him."

Jamie returned her a scathing look. "You wouldn't be *scared* would you?" he queried, with all the scorn of a bright eight-year-old for anything that could be thought remotely cissy.

"Yes, I would," she confessed without hesitation. "I've too healthy a regard for my own skin to want to dash around at that sort of speed with only a tin box around me."

Jamie chuckled with laughter, and turned his attention back to the challenge of the EcoWarrior, the tip of his tongue between his teeth as he zapped out the greenhouse gasses to repair the hole in the ozone layer. It had been a gift from his Uncle Leo, who owned the company that made it.

Well, at least forewarned was forearmed, Maddy reflected wryly. In fact, she ought to have guessed that he would be here—if she had allowed herself to think about him; but the habit of refusing to let herself think about him had become deeply ingrained over the years. She became aware that her hands were clenching the wheel a little too tightly, and made a conscious effort to relax them. She could cope with meeting Leo Ratcliffe again.

The telephone call from her sister-in-law had come in the small hours of the morning. She still wasn't quite sure how she was supposed to feel. Jeremy, the husband she had walked out on nearly six years ago, was dead— killed in a skiing accident. Off-piste, of course, and in defiance of all the avalanche warnings; sensible caution had never been Jeremy's strong point—he had always lived as if he believed himself to be indestructible.

Yes, she was sad—sad for the thought of what might have been, if only the spoilt little boy she had married had ever been able to grow up. And sad for a man who at least had known how to enjoy life—albeit with such magnificent selfishness—who suddenly was not there any more. He hadn't even reached his thirtieth birthday.

She glanced down at the child by her side, his soft brown head bent in deep concentration over his game. So far he seemed to have taken the news quite well. But at just eight years old he was just getting to the age when a father was important to him—and whatever else she might have accused Jeremy of, she couldn't deny that he had tried to be a good one. Once a month, regular as clockwork, he had arrived to take his son down to Hadley Park for his weekend visit.

Hadley Park... Of course—the beautiful old house, barely beyond the suburbs of Manchester but seemingly a world away, would be Jamie's now. A wry smile curved her delicate mouth at the thought. Jeremy, whose family had owned it for generations, had always seen it as nothing but a millstone, while she had loved it. Unfortunately, after death duties had taken their toll, there wasn't likely to be much money left to keep it up, she reflected pragmatically. But it would be a shame to have to sell it.

The quiet roads out of Manchester had once been so familiar to her, and now they brought the memories flooding back. She hadn't been back to Hadley Park since the day she had walked away from the wreckage of her marriage.

It had been a tough decision at the time, to strike out on her own with a small child in tow—she'd had no family to back her, and no marketable skills that she'd known of to earn her living. But her marriage had been going wrong virtually from the beginning, and finding out that her husband was sleeping with her best friend had just been the last straw.

She had often wondered why he hadn't married Saskia in the first place. He had known her long before he had met herself—in fact it had been Sass who introduced them. And if not then, why not later? He had known that she would have willingly given him a divorce if he had wanted one, without any fuss or scandal. But perhaps he had had enough sense to realise that any relationship needed one partner, at least, to have their feet somewhere near the ground—he and Sass were far too much alike, both wanting to flit through life without any cares or responsibilities.

Looking back now, she could only shake her head in sorry amazement that she had been such a fool as ever to believe that he was cut out for marriage. Her only excuse was that she had been young, and Jeremy had seemed able to offer her something from which she had felt excluded ever since her parents had died—a sense of family, of being part of a world of warmth and brightness and laughter, of belonging...

And it hadn't all been a disaster, she mused reminiscently. There had been some happy times, especially at the beginning. And she had her son. A small smile curved her soft mouth. No, she couldn't regret everything about her marriage.

A new set of traffic lights had been installed at the crossroads, and she drew the car to a halt, pulling on the handbrake and tucking her thick wheat-blonde hair back behind one ear in a characteristic gesture. She wore it now in a neat jaw-length bob; it had been one of the first things she had had done when she had decided to leave Jeremy—to have her hair cut. It had amused her since to learn that most women did exactly the same thing when they were asserting their independence for the first time.

And she *was* independent, she reflected with some pride. The modest little house in Whythenshaw that she had managed to buy last year might not be Hadley Park, but she owed not one penny to the Ratcliffes. It was quite a struggle to keep up with the hefty repayments on the mortgage, but she had known from the start that she wouldn't be able to rely on any regular maintenance from Jeremy.

Besides, she preferred to manage alone, however difficult it was—Jeremy's family had never made any secret of their belief that she had married him for his money, and it was good to be proving them wrong. And she had discovered shortly after leaving him that she *did* have a marketable talent after all—arranging children's parties.

It had begun when she had put on a very small party for Jamie's third birthday, to help him make new friends in the playgroup he had just joined. It had been such a success that one of the other mums, who worked full-time, had asked her to do her little girl's birthday party as well. After that it had snowballed, and then she had been asked to do grown-up parties too—even weddings. She was kept very busy, but she loved every minute of it—who wouldn't, being paid to help people enjoy themselves?

The traffic lights changed to green and she turned left, driving on carefully through the village. Little had changed here, at least, she mused—the post office had closed, its windows boarded up, and the old-fashioned grocery had adapted itself grudgingly to the supermarket era, but after the cosmopolitan bustle of Manchester it had the air of having been locked in a time-warp for the past three decades.

The high stone wall that surrounded Hadley Park started just beyond the edge of the village. The massive wrought-iron gates stood open—in fact it looked as if the hinges were too rusted to allow them to close, she noticed as she drove through. There were more weeds and pot-holes in the drive than there used to be, too.

And then through the trees she caught her first glimpse of the house, and slowed the car to get a better look. She had almost forgotten how beautiful it was, set against a backdrop of rolling green hills that led up to the high, rugged tors of the Peak District in the far misty distance. Built in the reign of the first Elizabeth, the golden stone of its walls had been mellowed by centuries, and its roof-line was a jumble of gables and twisted chimney-pots against the crisp blue and white of the February sky.

Jamie glanced up from his game. "Oh, we're there," he remarked, with the philistine unconcern of a seven-year-old for the magnificent heritage which had now passed into his small hands. "Great—I'm starving!"

Maddy laughed, and, putting the elderly car in gear again, she rolled it forward, bringing it to a halt beside the wide stone steps that led up to the front door. Jamie, sure of his welcome, scrambled out, skipping up the steps as the door was opened by a matronly woman in a flowered cotton overall, who greeted him with a warm hug.

Maddy followed him a little more diffidently, glad of her leather shoulder-bag to clutch on to. But as she climbed the steps the housekeeper looked up, her kindly face wreathed in smiles. "Why, Mrs Ratcliffe! I wouldn't hardly have known you with your hair short like that! Come in, come in." She held the front door wide open, ushering Maddy inside. "Such a nasty shock it's been... Oh—I'm sorry..." She stopped herself awkwardly, glancing at Jamie, her eyebrows lifted in unspoken enquiry.

"It's all right, Mrs Harris—he knows," Maddy assured her quietly. "Thank you—it must have been an awful shock for you too." The housekeeper's eyes were still noticeably red, and she was clutching a rolled-up clump of damp paper tissue in her hand; she had known Jeremy since he had been Jamie's age.

"It was." Mrs Harris dabbed at her eyes. "I still can't quite make myself believe it—though I know there hasn't been any mistake. Well, young man," she added, turning to Jamie and pinning a bright smile in place. "Guess

what I'm going to do you for lunch. Your favourite—
Welsh rarebit. I didn't know what time you might get
down,'' she told Maddy. "And what with all the
upset..."

"Of course," Maddy assured her quickly. "I wouldn't
want you to go to any trouble—Welsh rarebit will suit
me fine."

"Mum, can I go down to the kitchen with Auntie
Peggy?" Jamie demanded eagerly. "I want to see Mrs
Tiggywinkle's kittens."

"Oh, there's only one left o'them now," Mrs Harris
told him. "The rest we found homes for."

A frown of disappointment crossed the small face, but
it quickly brightened. "Which one did you keep?" he
asked. "Was it the black one?"

"Of course—he's yours."

That news brought immediate delight. "I'm going to
call him Sooty. Daddy said—" He stopped abruptly, remembering. "Daddy said it was a good name," he finished, the wistful note in his voice tugging at Maddy's
heartstrings.

"It's an excellent name," she assured him gently—
though mentally noting that she would have appreciated
it if Jeremy had consulted her before bestowing the gift
on their son. "Why don't you run downstairs and find
him? I haven't seen him yet, and I'd love to meet him."

"I rather think," a dry voice spoke behind her, "this
is the animal you're looking for."

Maddy turned sharply, catching her breath. "Leo...
Oh, hello," she managed, struggling to recover before
anyone should notice the slip in her composure.
"I...wasn't expecting you to be here."

She found herself subjected to a mocking survey
from a pair of deep-set agate eyes—the same colour as

Jeremy's, she couldn't help remembering, but lacking his openness and warmth.

"Hello, Maddy—nice to see you again. It's been a long time," he remarked, pointedly failing to mention that since he had passed her on the road, and his car was parked outside, she could have reasonably assumed that he was in the house. "You'd better come into the library—we have things to discuss. Jamie, take this little pest downstairs where he belongs," he added, unhooking the tiny kitten's claws from the front of his shirt and holding him out to the boy. "He doesn't seem to understand that I haven't come here exclusively to provide him with entertainment."

Jamie gurgled with laughter, not at all intimidated. "Thanks, Uncle Leo. Sorry if he's been bothering you. I'll take him down to the kitchen and give him a saucer of milk." He took the kitten with care. "Look, Mum— what do you think of him?" he added excitedly.

"He's cute." She tickled the little creature's ear, and he rubbed his head against her finger before opening his tiny pink mouth in a wide yawn. "But I think he's tired now. Take him down and give him his milk, and then put him down to sleep for a while."

The child nodded solemnly, cradling his precious bundle in his arms as he bore it away.

"Two coffees, please, Peggy," Leo requested as he stood aside for Maddy to enter the library.

She stepped past him, just a little too conscious of him for comfort; she had always been too conscious of him, but she would have thought that after all these years she would be better able to handle it. It was probably just that she was to some extent in shock, and hadn't been expecting to see him here so soon.

She glanced around the comfortable room, taking in the details that had once been so familiar, noting the small changes. "The grandfather clock's gone."

"Well spotted," Leo responded, a sardonic inflexion in his voice. "I'm afraid you'll find that Jeremy's sold off quite a number of trinkets over the years—I hope there was nothing of special importance to you?"

"Not particularly." She forced herself to meet his eyes levelly. "I didn't know Jeremy had financial problems."

He shrugged his wide shoulders in casual disregard. "When didn't he have financial problems?" he returned. 'Annual income twenty pounds, annual expenditure twenty pounds eight and six...' I'm afraid my dear cousin had little idea of economy."

Maddy smiled wryly; she knew that had been true enough. Moving across the room, she sat down in the armchair beside the large fireplace—rather disappointingly occupied by a two-bar electric fire, instead of the glowing real log fire it seemed to warrant.

From beneath her lashes she studied the man opposite her, noting the details and changes in him, too. She hadn't seen him since she had left Jeremy, but the years didn't seem to have had much effect on him. There was a strong family likeness between the two men—but whereas in Jeremy the chiselled structure of high forehead and hard jaw had been somewhat softened by an easygoing nature and a taste for the good life, in his older cousin there was an uncompromising masculinity that was more than a little unnerving.

She could still remember the first time she had met him, as vividly as if it had been only yesterday. It had been Saskia's twenty-first birthday party, and she had announced just a few days previously that it was also to be her engagement party...

"Maddy! Oh, I'm so glad you could come!" Saskia's soft blue eyes glowed with gratitude as she threw open the front door and reached out an impulsive hand to draw Maddy into the house. "It wouldn't have seemed the same without you here."

Maddy laughed, shaking her head. "Don't be silly— you didn't think I'd miss your party, did you?" She held out a small parcel, wrapped in pretty paper. "Happy birthday."

"Oh, Maddy—you shouldn't have!" Saskia protested. "And you struggling by with just your grant...!"

"I can manage to fork out for the odd pressy for my best friend," Maddy assured her, indulgent of her friend's over-sensitive concern—it was something she still hadn't grown out of.

Occasionally, when they had been at school together, she had found Saskia's tendency to make a drama out of almost any minor incident more than a little irritating. But she had been too grateful for her friendship to let it come between them; all the other girls had looked down their noses at her, knowing that she only had a place at the expensive private boarding-school because her aunt was the deputy headmistress. They had had a thousand subtle ways of letting her know that she didn't belong, never failing to notice if she was wearing one of their cast-off pieces of school uniform, always talking about the ponies their doting parents had bought them, and later their cars.

"Ah, goody—you've brought your overnight bag," Saskia cried excitably. "I'll get Jepson to take it upstairs—Mummie's put you in the room right next to mine. It'll be such fun—just like rotten old Calderbrook, except without Miss Pikington stalking the corridors like something out of *Alien*!'

Maddy chuckled at the graphic simile. "Thank goodness for that! But I'll take my bag up myself, if you'll just tell me which room—I need to freshen up before I join the party."

"Oh, of course—I'm sorry, I never thought of it." Saskia looked stricken by such a lapse, but instantly brightened. "I'll come up with you—I'm dying to catch up with all your news. How are you enjoying your teaching course?"

"It's fun—especially the teaching practice. I had a class of six-year-olds this term—they really keep you on your toes!"

Saskia shuddered theatrically. "Ugh—rather you than me! Children aren't my cup of tea, I'm afraid—the less I have to do with them, the better."

Maddy glanced at her in surprise. "But surely you're going to have some of your own when you get married?" she protested. "What about your fiancé? Doesn't he want them?"

Saskia shook her head. "No, thank goodness!" They had reached the second floor, and a long, quiet corridor with a gleaming parquet floor. It must take ages to polish, Maddy mused—not that Saskia's mother had to do it herself. Saskia threw open a door, showing Maddy into a spacious bedroom, beautifully furnished with repro-duction antiques, with a thick-piled rose-pink carpet and matching velvet swags at the windows.

"The bathroom's through there," Saskia pointed out. "Is it OK?"

Maddy glanced around, her delicate mouth curving into a wry smile—it was about three times the size of the tiny little study-bedroom she had at college, and in-finitely more elegant. "It's fine," she responded, barely suppressing the sardonic note in her voice.

Saskia bounced on the bed, as excited as a child. "Hurry up and get ready," she urged. "I'm dying to introduce you to Leo."

"Leo?" Maddy slanted her friend a teasing look. "It was all very quick, this engagement—how long have you known him?"

"Oh, ages! He's practically family—by marriage, anyway. He's been abroad for the past few years, though—he only came back at Christmas. So I grabbed him before he could get away again!" she added with a giggle.

"So what's he like? Tell me all about him."

"He's in computers—he's started up his own company," Saskia told her, her eyes bright. "He's fabulously rich—and he drives an Aston Martin!"

Maddy, brushing her long hair in the mirror, glanced past her own reflection to that of her friend. Saskia's shallowness was something else she had grown to tolerate over the years, and she wasn't really surprised to hear her describe someone in terms of his bank balance or the car he drove; but as criteria for choosing a husband they seemed to her to leave a lot to be desired. She was half inclined to feel a little sorry for the unknown Leo.

She looked back at her own reflection, wryly aware that beside the sensational moiré satin evening number Saskia was wearing her own simple black dress looked what it was—inexpensive, and several years old. But she so rarely wore an evening dress that it hadn't seemed worth spending the money on a new one. Her only jewelry was the tiny gold locket her mother had left her, with miniature photographs of her parents inside.

At school, the differences between their backgrounds had never been quite so noticeable, she mused wistfully. It hadn't been the money so much—though that had been the most obvious factor—but that Saskia had had a home, and a family—somewhere to belong. Maddy hadn't had that since her parents had died—her Aunt Helen was her only family, the exclusive Calderbrook boarding-school her only home.

And, apart from the fact that they were both blonde, they were very different types. Saskia was a spring blonde, with baby-fine flaxen hair and a delicate, rosebud prettiness, while the image that gazed back at her showed rather stronger features—a chin that had learned to take life's hard knocks, a nose that bordered on the aquiline, and eyes of a smoky grey. She was taller, too—though they probably still took the same dress-size.

She gave her hair a last flick with the brush—she had grown it long because she couldn't afford to keep having it cut, and it was now almost down to her waist—and turned to Saskia with a warm smile. "OK—I'm ready," she announced breezily. "Lead on, Macduff!"

"Great!" exclaimed Saskia, skipping to her feet. "Come on, then."

Together they descended the stairs to the ground floor. The sound of music and conversation drifted up to them before they reached it—more guests had arrived while they had been upstairs, it seemed. Maddy felt her stomach clench with tension; she had come for Saskia's sake, but she knew she didn't really belong in a gathering like this—as she had never belonged at school. She had always been the "charity girl".

The house was large; the staircase descended in a sweep to an imposing entrance hall, with rooms opening on each side of it. As they reached the foot a devastatingly handsome young man in an immaculately cut dinner jacket that moulded an impressive breadth of shoulder stepped out from one of the rooms, and, catching sight of Saskia, immediately swept her up in a hug, lifting her off her feet and swinging her round.

"Sassy! The love of my life! You're looking absolutely ravishing tonight—good enough to eat."

Maddy watched, amused and somewhat relieved. She had been a little worried, hearing Saskia's pragmatic description of her intended, that her friend had entered into this engagement for all the wrong reasons. But she was pleasantly surprised; no one could mistake the attraction between these two. It crossed her mind briefly that he seemed a little young for the high-powered businessman Saskia had described—but then computers was apparently a business for young whiz-kids, if the papers and television were to be believed.

Something made her sense that she was being watched, and she glanced across the hall. Another man had followed the first into the hall, and as she met his dark eyes an odd little shiver of recognition struck her, although she knew that she had never seen him before in her life—unless it had been in her dreams... But the next instant she realised why he had seemed so familiar—he looked so much like Saskia's fiancé that he had to be his older brother.

The couple in the hall stopped spinning, laughing and breathless, and Saskia struck her fiancé a playful blow on the chest. "Wretch—you've made me giddy now. Anyway, I want you to meet my very best friend."

Brown eyes, as mischievous and friendly as a puppy's, smiled up at Maddy, and at once he let Saskia go, darting up the stairs. "Oh boy—you're gorgeous!" he flattered outrageously. "Sass, you never told me your friend was so beautiful."

Maddy blushed, laughing at his teasing—but a little wary, anxious not to appear to be giving him any inappropriate encouragement. She held out her hand, smiling up at him. "Hello—I've been looking forward to meeting you," she said. "Saskia's told me a lot about you."

His dark eyebrows arched in surprise, and he chuckled richly. "Really? Not the truth, I hope, Sass? That'd ruin my chances before I'd even got started!"

Maddy flashed him a look of sharp discouragement, drawing her hand from his, but Saskia was laughing merrily. "Don't be a loon, Jeremy—Maddy's far too good for you."

Maddy blinked at her in bewilderment. "Jeremy? But... I thought..."

"*This* is Leo."

The other man had strolled forward, and Saskia linked her hands through his arm, holding on to him as if he was some kind of trophy. Maddy felt an odd sensation, like the twang of a loose guitar-string, way out of tune, deep in the pit of her stomach. But he was smiling up at her pleasantly, holding out his hand, and she put hers in it briefly.

"Hello, Maddy—I've heard a great deal about you," he greeted her. "This young reprobate, for whom I have the misfortune to be frequently mistaken, is my cousin."

It was easy to see how such a mistake could be made at a first glance—though not, Maddy concluded, at a second. Leo was older, though it was hard to tell by how much—five years, maybe? Both men were tall, though Leo had the advantage of maybe an inch or two—his shoulders were perhaps a little wider, too. They both had dark hair, almost black, but Jeremy wore his longer, curling around his ears—and he had the readier smile.

He was laughing now, flattered by his cousin's epithet. "He's got the brains, but I've got the charm," he

confided to Maddy. "Hey, you haven't got a drink yet.
Come on, stick with me, babe—I'll take care of you."

She allowed herself to be swept away, into the hubbub
of the party. Jeremy found her a glass of champagne,
and began introducing her to people. He seemed to know
everyone there, and clearly he was extremely popular—
with the men as well as the women. Held at his side by
a casual arm around her waist, Maddy felt as if she had
been caught up in the sparkling aura of a flashing comet.

It was a wonderful feeling, as intoxicating as the sweet,
bubbly champagne she was sipping. Everyone wanted to
know her, no one seemed to care about her shabby
dress—in fact it almost began to seem as if it was she
who was the most stylish, they who were overdressed.
Jeremy's laughter was infectious, and his outrageous
compliments flattering enough to cause even the most
solidly grounded common sense to waver.

As dusk descended the garden was lit up with brightly
coloured paper lanterns, strung from the branches of
the trees. A marquee had been set up on the lawn, and
a local band was playing loud rock music for people to
dance to. Breathless, Maddy let Jeremy spin her round
in a wild jive, her long hair flying, as his friends cheered
them on.

She had never enjoyed herself so much in her life. It
had always seemed as if she was out of step; at school
she had been the charity girl, in hand-me-down clothes,
while ironically at college she had found that the manners
and speech she had acquired at school tended to set her
apart from her peers, who were inclined to regard her
as a snob. But tonight she felt for the first time as if she
was really accepted.

The only fly in the ointment was Saskia; catching sight
of her hovering beside the French window that led into

the house, Maddy was surprised to see a petulant expression marring that pretty face. A stab of guilt struck through her; it was Saskia's engagement party, and here was she—Maddy—at the centre of attention. As soon as she could, she slipped away from Jeremy's side and hurried over to her friend.

"Sassy—what's wrong?" she asked gently. She glanced around. "Where's Leo?"

Saskia shrugged her slim shoulders in a gesture of sulky indifference. "In Daddy's den—he had an important call from New York."

"Oh, what a pity—spoiling the party for him like that," Maddy protested. "Still, I suppose he had to take it if it was really important."

"Oh, it doesn't matter," Saskia asserted dismissively. "You seem to be enjoying yourself, anyway. Watch out for Jeremy, though—he's a devil. If you're not careful you'll end up as just another name in his little black book."

Maddy looked down at her friend in astonishment—surely that couldn't be a note of jealousy she detected in her voice? But then Saskia sighed wistfully, tucking her hand confidingly into Maddy's arm.

"I don't seem to have had a chance to chat to you all evening," she protested plaintively. "And it's months since I've seen you."

"Oh, Sassy—I'm sorry." It was quite true, of course—it was Saskia who had invited her, and it had been selfish of her to go off with Jeremy all evening. "Come on, let's go inside for a little while," she coaxed. "It's a little quieter in there."

Saskia complied willingly enough, but within a few moments of them sitting down in the spacious drawing-room Jeremy came in search of them. "So this is where you're hiding,'' he declared, perching on the arm of the settee beside Maddy.

Saskia giggled, unmistakably flirting with him. "Oh, Jeremy—we weren't hiding. We just popped in here for a breather—it's such a dreadful crush!"

"Rubbish!" he insisted. "Time enough when you're middle-aged to take a breather—come and dance!"

Saskia jumped up at once, laughingly accepting the invitation—though Maddy had thought it had been directed to her. But then these two were clearly old friends. And Sassy deserved to enjoy herself—after all, it was her party. As Jeremy caught at her hand to drag her along with them she shook her head, smiling to soften the refusal, following them more slowly.

The far end of the terrace was in shadow, and she retreated there for a while, watching the dancing a little wistfully—without Jeremy at her side, it seemed as if she had become invisible again. That familiar tug of envy twisted inside her; she was on the outside, as usual, unable to get in. Even Saskia had only really been friends with her because she had few friends herself—most people weren't prepared to tolerate that sometimes irritating affectation...

"Not dancing?"

She glanced up in surprise to find Leo Ratcliffe at her side. "Oh... No, not just for the moment," she managed a little awkwardly.

"I found this in the drawing-room—I believe it's yours."

He held out a small, heart-shaped gold locket, and Maddy gasped in shock, her hand flying automatically to her bare throat. "Oh, my goodness—yes, it is! Thank you." She took it from him, agitation making her hands shake. She might have lost it, and it was the only thing she had... "The clasp isn't broken—I must have not fastened it properly. It was a good job it slipped off here—I might have lost it on the train..."

And never seen it again. The bleakness of that thought brought tears to her eyes, but she quickly blinked them back under cover of refastening the chain around her neck—being extra careful this time that it was fastened properly.

"It's a pretty little thing," he remarked, lifting it on his finger to study the fine flower pattern wrought into the gold.

"Yes..."

Suddenly she became aware of how close she was to him. There was a faint, musky, male kind of scent about him—not an aftershave, she was sure, but the unique scent of his own skin. It seemed to have a strange effect on her senses, and when she looked up she found herself gazing into his eyes. Deep-set brown eyes—not quite the same colour as Jeremy's, she realised now, but a shade darker, and intriguingly flecked with gold...

"Leo! You said you'd only be ten minutes, and you've been gone half an hour!" Saskia's petulant voice shattered the fleeting spell as she dragged Jeremy up the steps of the terrace. "Come and dance with me."

He shook his head, smiling down at her indulgently. "In this crush? No, thank you. Come and get something to eat instead."

For a moment Saskia looked rebellious, but then she smiled sweetly, tucking her hands into his arms and stretching up on tiptoe to put a kiss on his cheek. "All right," she conceded, her sapphire-blue eyes aglow with adoration. "If that's what *you* want."

Maddy watched them walk away. Was that how it always was with them? They did whatever he wanted?

She had quite been beginning to like him—almost, even, to envy Saskia a little bit. It had even crossed her mind to wonder why a man of such apparent intelligence would choose to marry a featherbrain like Sass—fond as she was of her, she could describe her in no other way. But apparently he was one of those men who wanted a sweet, biddable little wife, who would hang on his every word and think he was absolutely wonderful. She was aware of feeling just a little disappointed in him.

But Jeremy was demanding her attention, dragging her out on to the dance-floor. She did enjoy dancing, and she couldn't help but enjoy Jeremy's company. And as the evening drew on, and the music slowed, she found that she enjoyed being in his arms, and being kissed by him. And, if her mind occasionally wandered to thoughts of Leo, she could remind herself that Jeremy was every bit as attractive, and certainly more fun. And he wasn't engaged to her best friend.

CHAPTER TWO

"WHAT... was it you wanted to discuss, Leo?" Maddy enquired, relieved to find that her voice was now completely under control again.

With a wave of his hand he indicated the piles of bills and documents on the desk and on the floor around it, stuffed into shoe-boxes and old brown envelopes— Jeremy had never had much patience with paperwork. "This. I've been trying to go through Jeremy's papers and see if there's anything that needs my immediate attention, but it's the biggest mess I've ever seen."

The note of censure in his voice stung her into sharp annoyance. "I'm sure there's nothing that can't wait another few days," she retorted. "Why are you going through it anyway? Shouldn't that be left to the executors of the estate?"

"I *am* one of the executors," he responded evenly. "You're the other. We've also been named as joint trustees. Everything's been left to Jamie, naturally— although you're to have a lifetime annuity—and there are a few small gifts to the staff."

"Oh..." A lump had risen to her throat, and her eyes filled up with tears; it was so sad to think of Jeremy drawing up his will, cheerfully expecting that it would be many years before it would be needed. And it was typical of his generosity to have remembered the staff— but why on earth had he had to make Leo her co-trustee?

The housekeeper's arrival with the coffee gave her a few moments to regain her composure. She should have guessed, of course, that Jeremy would have wanted Leo to administer his estate; he had always looked up to his older cousin—maybe even been slightly in awe of him. And he hadn't been aware that Maddy would have preferred not to have too much to do with him.

Leo brought over a small table, set it down beside her chair and put her coffee-cup on it before seating himself on the opposite side of the fireplace. "How has Jamie taken it?" he enquired.

"Oh... He seems OK. Well, you saw him. He's old enough to understand, but not old enough to really take it in properly. He knows it means he won't be seeing his daddy again, but I suppose it'll be a while before the realisation sinks in."

"Yes." Leo's voice had thickened. "It will be for me, too."

"For all of us," she mused sadly.

Leo's cold laughter startled her. "Oh, come on," he protested, on a note of cynical mockery. "Don't start playing the broken-hearted widow. All it's done for you is save you the bother of getting a divorce."

"I beg your pardon?" Her eyes flashed with frosty indignation. "For your information, I was still very fond of Jeremy. And if I'd wanted a divorce, I could have had one years ago."

"Not without Jeremy's consent," he countered. "You walked out on him, remember? As the guilty party, you could only sit it out for the full five years."

She stared at him, struggling to regain sufficient control over her voice to answer him. "Don't you think I may perhaps have had good reason?" she queried with fine understatement.

Those agate eyes were hard and unforgiving. "You knew what he was like when you married him," he asserted disparagingly. "It didn't seem to matter to you then. You just wanted the sort of lifestyle you thought he could give you—the chance to mix with the county set, go to all the country house parties. But marriage vows are for better or worse, you know—not to turn your back on just because things don't turn out to be quite the bed of roses you were expecting."

Maddy felt her cheeks go from white to deep scarlet. He didn't know—Jeremy had never told him about Saskia. Of course not, she reflected wryly; even though that hopelessly misconceived engagement had ended inside of three months, Jeremy would have been reluctant to let his cousin know that he was having an affair with his ex-fiancée.

And she could hardly tell him now, she realised in the next instant; he probably wouldn't believe her, and it would just seem to him that she was trying to off-load the blame on to Jeremy when he could no longer defend himself. Besides, what did it matter to her what he thought of her? Once, maybe—but that was a long time ago. Now she only had to think about what was best for Jamie. She had to work with Leo over the administration of the estate—it would be best if personal feelings didn't come into it at all.

"What happened between Jeremy and I is none of your business," she informed him, her voice stiff with dignity. "But neither of us particularly wanted a divorce—it wasn't as if either of us was in any hurry to marry again. And besides, it was better for Jamie to leave things as they were. It was a perfectly amicable arrangement."

He lifted one dark eyebrow in frank scepticism, but shrugged the discussion aside with a lift of his wide shoulders. "Well, I suppose it's all somewhat academic

now, anyway," he remarked coldly. "It's the future that
we have to think about. I've made a list of the people
who will need to be notified about the funeral
arrangements..."

"Oh, have you?" she retorted in sharp annoyance.
"Don't you think perhaps you should have consulted
me? I am the next of kin, you know."

Anger, barely restrained, flared in his eyes. "Don't
get competitive about it," he warned, his voice quiet with
menace. "There's only one person who'll suffer if we
make enemies of each other, and that's your son."

She drew in a sharp breath; was that merely a reminder, or a warning? But he was right, of course—they
were going to have to co-operate with each other in order
to ensure that Jamie's inheritance would be worthwhile.
And, more than that, it wouldn't be good for him to
have them arguing over his head; like his father, he
seemed to have an inordinate regard for his "Uncle Leo"
—most times after his monthly visits to Hadley Park he
had had as much to say about Leo as about Jeremy. And
the fact that Leo was the creator of his beloved
EcoWarrior, as well as a number of other cult computer-
game figures, was enough to elevate him to the status
almost of a demi-god.

Drawing in a long, steadying breath, she inclined her
head in acknowledgement. "All right," she conceded
evenly. "May I see the list?"

He walked over to the desk and brought her back a
sheet of paper, with a long list of names neatly written
out in his handsome script—another way in which he
had differed from Jeremy, she reflected, recalling her
husband's lazy scrawl.

"That seems OK," she murmured; she knew most of
the names on the list, and none of them were unex-

pected. She had known Saskia's name would be on it, of course—she was family, her brother being married to Jeremy's older sister Julia. Yes, Saskia would be there, weeping touchingly for her childhood friend—and Maddy would be the only one who would know that she was in truth an adulterous little bitch who had wrecked her best friend's marriage.

"You're sure?" Those deep-set agate eyes had noted the tautness of her jaw. "Is there anyone you think I—*we*—should add?"

"No, I don't think so," she responded coolly. "You're suggesting that the funeral should be next week?"

"Yes. I would have gone for Friday, but it may be better to delay it, just in case there are any difficulties arising out of the inquest."

"Why should there be?" she queried, surprised. "I thought it was a quite straightforward skiing accident."

He shrugged his wide shoulders. "Almost certainly— but, nevertheless, the authorities will have to be sure that there was no question of...anything else. Like whether he was drunk."

"Drunk? Don't be ridiculous! Jeremy could be a little wild at times, but he never drank too much."

"How do you know?" Leo countered, a hard edge in his voice. "What would you know of his state of mind these past five years—what would you care? You saw him once a month when he came to fetch Jamie for his visit and brought him back."

She stared at him, her hands shaking slightly. "Are you saying that he'd become an alcoholic?"

He shook his head impatiently. "No, I'm not. But I do know he was unhappy. He was still in love with you— maybe if you'd still been around..."

"Yes?" Maddy's jaw was clenched tightly in anger. "Maybe if I'd still been around, what? He might not have had the accident—is that what you were going to say? That's it's all my fault?"

"No, of course not," he rapped back. "It just...might have steadied him down a little..."

"I already had one child to think about," she retorted hotly. "I couldn't cope with two." Fulminating grey eyes clashed with agate; Maddy could feel herself trembling—it was rare for her to be so close to losing her temper, and it was a feeling she didn't like.

She was the first to look away. Leo was right, to some extent—she had married Jeremy for all the wrong reasons. Oh, she had been deeply fond of him—but she had never been in love with him. She had let him spin her into a whirlwind romance, dazzled by his good looks and his charm, and by the aching need inside her to fill the loneliness of her life. And because the man she had fallen instantly in love with had already been spoken for.

But she had kept that last fact a secret for almost nine years. It had been a painful irony to learn, on returning from their crazy honeymoon jaunt around Africa, that Leo and Saskia had ended their engagement just two weeks after her own wedding.

Not that it would really have made any difference, she acknowledged. Leo had made it abundantly clear from the beginning that, like the rest of the family, he disapproved of his cousin's marriage. She did have some sympathy with their view that at twenty-one he had been far too young, but nothing could have been further from their belief that she had married him in order to claw her way a few rungs up the social ladder.

Leo sighed, and shrugged his wide shoulders in weary impatience. "Perhaps this isn't the best time to discuss it," he conceded. "I understand you'll be staying for a few days—Julia has arranged for you to have the Yellow Room. Jamie can go in the nursery, of course, as usual."

"Thank you." So Jeremy's sister was here already, organising everything in her usual high-handed fashion. Maddy was surprised that they had even bothered to suggest she came down—between the two of them, they seemed to be making all the decisions. But then what else had she expected? They were, after all, Ratcliffes; everyone else was supposed to fall into step with them.

A tap at the door heralded the housekeeper's return, to announce that lunch was ready. "Shall I bring it up to the morning-room?" she suggested. "You won't want the big dining-room."

Maddy was tempted to say that she would prefer to come down to the warm kitchen, but Leo had already agreed that the morning-room would be the most suitable, so she kept her mouth shut. But if he and his cousin Julia thought she was still the diffident young girl who had come into their family all those years ago, they could be in for a surprise. She had no intention of letting herself be pushed around—and no intention of letting them interfere in her son's inheritance.

It was strange to be back, Maddy mused as she stood at the window of her bedroom, gazing out over the wood-fringed parkland of the estate. The house was much as she remembered it—though she couldn't help noticing that there were even more minor repairs that needed to be done, a few of them now becoming quite urgent if the fabric of the building was to be preserved.

It was a pity Jeremy hadn't taken his responsibility to the family seat more seriously. She had tried to persuade him often enough, but it had usually led to an ar-

gument—he preferred to spend his money on cars and
parties and having a good time. The income from the
land that went with the estate—farm tenancies, mostly—
had barely been enough to support such an extravagant
lifestyle even then. His own father's death, a couple of
years before she had met him, had already taken quite
a toll in death duties—a second charge now, not much
more than ten years later, could well prove to be the last
straw.

Which could mean that there was no alternative but
to sell the house, or hand it over to the National Trust—
if they would take it. But she didn't want to do that—
coming back here had reminded her of how important
Hadley Park was to her. It was more than just a house—
much more...

Unconsciously she lifted her hand to touch the tiny
gold locket she always wore at her throat. It was the only
thing that had come out of the fire that had destroyed
her own home and killed her parents. She had been just
twelve years old, and had survived only because of the
odd irony that she had been in hospital having her tonsils
out.

In that one night her whole childhood—all her memories, every photograph, every toy she had had since she
was a baby—had disappeared. Without a history, she
had always felt a strange, lingering sense of detachment,
as if she was somehow a loose thread in the fabric of
the human race—left dangling, not properly woven in.

It was a feeling that had to some extent gone away
with the birth of her son, but she had never forgotten
it. And now that she was back here, in the house that
had belonged to his Ratcliffe ancestors for so many generations, she remembered how determined she had been
that he should know that he had a history—it was here,

in these old stone walls and the deep, solid earth that they stood upon. This was his birthright, and she was going to hold on to it for him—no matter what it took.

But she was going to have to think of a way to generate sufficient income to keep it going, she mused wryly. And that would be no easy task. It was rather too small, and lacked the kudos of real aristocratic connections, to attract many visitors if it were opened to the public. And she had no desire to fill the gardens with wild animals or fairground attractions.

As she stood there, gazing absently out at the garden as it waited for the touch of spring to ripen the green buds of the daffodils that grew in wild profusion in all the flowerbeds, her mind slipped back to that encounter with Leo. Seeing him again had brought back so many memories. She had thought she had put all that behind her, but, like lumber in the attic, she had never sorted it out properly, and now that the door had been opened again it had all come tumbling out...

It had all happened so quickly that she had barely had time to think. Jeremy had proposed to her just three days after Saskia's party, and now, less than two months later, here she was, walking up the aisle in a romantic dress of white lace, on the arm of Saskia's father who had stood in for her own to give her away.

She had tried to persuade Jeremy to wait a little—after all, she was only nineteen, and he was barely twenty-one. But he had brushed all her protests aside, sweeping her along on the tide of his own impetuousness—it was hard to believe that all this was really happening.

And then she glanced up towards the altar, and saw the two men standing there—so very much alike to look at, so different in every other way... Her heart gave a sudden thud, almost taking her breath away. She hadn't seen Leo since the night of the party—he had been away on business—but she knew that Jeremy had written to him and begged him to come home in time to be his best man.

She hadn't been unduly worried about his return— had managed to convince herself that it had been no more than her imagination, that reaction she had felt the first time she had seen him. But here it was again— a thousand times stronger. Those deep-set, agate-coloured eyes met hers, and she felt as if her bones were melting.

But it was wrong—it shouldn't be happening. She was in love with Jeremy... wasn't she? Confusion swirled in her brain as she stared at the two of them: Jeremy, so boyishly handsome, his eyes alight with happiness as he waited for his bride—and Leo, a faintly cynical smile curving that firm, sensuous mouth, the arrogant set of his wide shoulders reminding her that the downside of all that magnetic male charisma was a personality that expected to have everything its own way.

Unfortunately, it wasn't exactly a good moment to pause for a little calm reflection—her slight hesitation had been noticed, and everyone was looking at her with avid curiosity. She could hardly request a postponement of the wedding on the grounds that she wasn't sure if she was marrying the right man. And besides, Leo was engaged to the girl who was today her own bridesmaid— an engagement sealed with an enormous diamond that must have cost a fortune.

Drawing in a deep, steadying breath, she forced herself to go on. As she drew to Jeremy's side he smiled down at her, taking her hand warmly in his, and she told herself it would be all right—it was just a last-minute attack of nerves. But she was glad to be able to hide behind the heavy lace fall of her veil as the vicar began to welcome the congregation, all too acutely aware of the man at the very edge of her vision . . . as he had been at the edge of her mind for the past two months.

Perhaps it was just that Jeremy had spoken about him so much—he was obviously very fond of his older cousin, maybe even a little in awe of him. It had been Leo, the captain of the most successful rugby team in the history of the school, Leo who had got a First at Oxford, Leo who knew everything there was to know about computers . . .

And, after all, there had been nothing in his behaviour that first night to suggest that he had been struck in the same way she had—he had shown nothing beyond a mere friendly politeness towards his fiancée's best friend. And though she knew that her slender height and long blonde hair attracted a lot of male attention—not always the kind of attention she liked—she was certainly not vain enough to suppose that the effect would be universal. She was just being stupid.

The vicar was reciting the vows, and she repeated them in a whisper. Jeremy squeezed her hand encouragingly, smiling down at her, and she realised with a small stab of guilt that he had completely misinterpreted the reason for her nervousness. But she meant what she was saying—she really did. "Forsaking all others . . ."

And then Leo stepped forward to hand Jeremy the ring, and though she tried with all the strength of her will to resist, she couldn't help but lift her eyes to his— to find him watching her, his dark gaze seeming to see right into her soul. He knew—even behind the thick lace of her veil she couldn't hide from him. He had never even touched her, and yet she belonged to him . . .

At last the ceremony was over, and they all crowded into the tiny vestry to sign the register. As soon as they were inside, Jeremy caught her round the waist and swung her around in a wild polka, bumping heedlessly into the table and the walls, culminating in a deep, steaming kiss.

"Hello, Mrs Ratcliffe!" he proclaimed as at last he let her go.

She laughed, breathless, her cheeks faintly tinged with pink; at least everyone would assume her blush was one of bridal modesty—except, perhaps, for Leo. But she couldn't risk letting herself glance in his direction—better to try to pretend that he wasn't there.

Saskia, pretty as a picture in her pink bridesmaid dress, hurried over to help her straighten her veil. "Oh, isn't it wonderful!" she declared, her sapphire-blue eyes dancing as she kissed her cheek. "Now you're really almost my sister, instead of just my best friend."

Maddy smiled; that was what she had always wanted—to be part of a family, to belong. And, though she knew that Jeremy's family hadn't approved of the speed with which it had all happened, now that they were married and they saw how happy Jeremy was they would surely come round to accepting her.

They were all gathering around her—Saskia's parents, and her brother Nigel, who was married to Jeremy's elder sister Julia—kissing her and wishing her well. Even Julia managed some sort of smile, and a dry peck on her cheek, though it seemed to cost her dear; Maddy responded to her as warmly as she could—that was a relationship she was going to have to work very hard at.

And then Leo was there, slanting his cousin a teasing glance. "Do you mind if I kiss the bride?" he asked, an inflection of something Maddy couldn't quite interpret in his voice.

"Of course," Jeremy responded cheerfully. "Best man's privilege."

Maddy stiffened, every nerve-fibre in her body stretched taut as Leo turned to her, his hands resting lightly on her shoulders as he drew her towards him. A faintly mocking smile glinted in those agate eyes. "Jeremy's a very lucky man to have such a beautiful bride," he murmured. "No wonder he was in such a hurry to tie the knot."

"Th—thank you," she stammered, hoping he wouldn't detect the agitated racing of her heartbeat.

He bent his head and his mouth brushed over hers, warm and firm, just as she had known it would be. Her heart creased in pain; she wasn't supposed to feel like this—she wasn't allowed to. Longing to have him hold her close, she drew back quickly, her cheeks deeply tinged with pink, her eyes unable to meet his.

Fortunately no one seemed to have noticed anything untoward—Julia's small son Aubrey, frustrated at not being the centre of attention, had chosen that moment to throw a minor tantrum, and Jeremy was enjoying a bridegroom's liberties with the chief bridesmaid, who was giggling as he kissed her.

With a supreme effort of will, she pulled herself together. It was just the excitement of the day, the crazy rush of it all, she told herself firmly—it really wasn't surprising that she hardly knew if she was on her head or her heels. But she would be very careful from now on not to let Leo get too close—she wasn't sure quite what it was about him that had such a disturbing effect on her, but she wanted no repetition of it.

Even so, it was a strain to get through the rest of the day—smiling for endless photographs, standing beside Jeremy at the entrance to the huge marquee that had been erected in the garden of his house, greeting an endless line of guests, most of whom she had never even seen before. She sensed that they were all looking down their noses at her, convinced that Jeremy had married beneath him; she was grateful to Saskia for being there, conspicuously loyal, telling everyone that they had been at school together.

Then there was the lavish wedding-breakfast, and the speeches, and then everything was swiftly cleared away so that the guests could dance to the music of a local band. As the afternoon wore on into evening Maddy began to develop a splitting headache; the marquee was hot and stuffy, and she was desperate for a breath of fresh air. Jeremy was dancing with one of his aunts, and no one noticed as she slipped quietly away.

The gardens of Hadley Park were beautiful—a little neglected in places, with trails of bright blue periwinkle growing wild among the flowerbeds, and honeysuckle scrambling all along the broken stone parapet that ran around the terrace at the back of the house, its sweet fragrance filling the air. The sky had turned a soft dark blue, streaked with high magenta clouds as the sun sank below the horizon.

Wandering into a secluded corner, she found a wooden pergola, covered with climbing roses. There was a rustic seat inside and she sat down wearily, closing her eyes. Her mind was a turmoil of confusion; had she been wrong to marry Jeremy? She had genuinely believed she was in love with him, and yet... Maybe she had let herself be swept up by his ebullient personality, feeling for the first time in her life that she was on the inside of one of those charmed circles she had always envied—and maybe she had mistaken gratitude for love...

A sound close by brought her eyes sharply open—as Leo stepped into the pergola. Startled, she jumped to her feet—and gave a little cry of horror as the puffed sleeve of her dress caught on a stray rose-thorn. "Oh...damn and blast it!" she muttered fiercely under her breath, twisting around as she tried to free herself.

"Hold still," he advised in that dry, sardonic tone. "If you keep pulling at it like that you'll rip it."

Her heart gave an uncomfortable thud and began to race rapidly as he leaned close to her and carefully disentangled the delicate silk from the thorn. "Th—thank you," she managed, hoping he wouldn't notice the slight tremor in her voice. "I...just came out for a few minutes—I couldn't breathe in there."

"I wondered what you were doing out here all by yourself," he remarked. "Beginning to pall already, is it?"

She glanced up at him in surprise, taken aback by the hard glint in those agate eyes. "I'm sorry?" she queried, frowning.

"I wonder if you will be?" he mused, deliberately misunderstanding. "Unfortunately I'm inclined to think it's my impetuous young cousin who'll be the one to be sorry. You know what they say—'Marry in haste, repent at leisure'. And you certainly married in haste."

She glared up at him in indignant fury. "Yes, we did," she retorted defensively. "But so what? Jeremy loves me."

"Oh, I've no doubt of that," Leo drawled, an inflexion of mocking cynicism in his voice. "He's written to me more in the past two months than he ever has in his life—every letter singing your praises. But I'm left in some doubt about you." His eyes flickered down over her in icy contempt. "Some of my more naïve relatives seem to think you've trapped him into matrimony by getting pregnant, but I think they've underestimated your subtlety."

"I...I don't know what you mean," she protested, bewildered.

"Don't you?" His smile was hard, not reaching his eyes. "Strange—I'm sure you're a very clever girl. Clever enough to know that getting pregnant would have been exceedingly risky—besotted as he is, there'd be no guarantee that Jeremy would do the decent thing. So you played an even more old-fashioned trick; and very effectively, too—particularly with someone like Jeremy, who is regrettably not very good at being patient when he wants something. I just hope you feel the prize is worth the effort."

"Of course I do!" Anger lent her voice a note of conviction it might otherwise have lacked. "I...love Jeremy—very much."

He lifted one dark eyebrow a fraction of an inch—but it spoke volumes. "Well, there's some reassurance in that, I suppose," he conceded coolly. "Though whether it will stand the test of time—and harsh reality—remains to be seen."

"Why shouldn't it?" she demanded, her voice ragged.

He lifted his wide shoulders in a cynical shrug. "Well, for one thing there's the matter of Jerry's income. No doubt he's given you the impression that there are money-trees growing here in the garden, but I'm afraid you'll find that the true picture isn't quite so rosy. Oh, there'll be more than enough to keep you in a reasonable degree of comfort, given a little practical economy. Unfortunately he's far too young to have any sense of responsibility.''

''Maybe that's the way you see it,'' she countered caustically. ''But you could be wrong, you know—maybe he's got more sense than you give him credit for.''

''Maybe,'' he conceded. ''But I wouldn't put it to the test too quickly, if I were you.'' Those hard eyes slid down quite deliberately over the beaded bodice of her dress to note the slenderness of her waist, his meaning insolently plain. ''Let him have his fun for a few years first.''

Maddy glared up at him, her hand positively itching to slap that arrogant face. ''That's none of your business!'' she protested hotly.

''Perhaps not,'' he acknowledged, an unmistakable note of warning in his voice. ''But I'm strangely fond of my young cousin—I wouldn't like to see him hurt.''

She felt her cheeks flame scarlet. ''What makes you think I'd hurt him?'' she demanded, her voice taut with agitation. ''I told you—I love him.''

''Do you?'' The chill in his eyes made her shiver. ''I wonder? I can't help feeling that if you were really that much in love with him, you wouldn't have been able to hold out quite so easily—you'd have gone to bed with him.''

This time she really did slap him—or at least she tried. But he was too quick for her, catching her wrist in a vice-like grip. Her eyes filled with tears of pain as his steely fingers dug into her dedicate skin. ''Let me go,'' she pleaded, all too acutely aware of the quivering response that was generating inside her; being so close to him, breathing the subtle musky scent of his skin, was affecting her in a way that she didn't know how to control.

Those agate eyes were gazing down into hers, the amber lights in their depths seeming to mesmerise her. "Because you're not quite the ice-princess you pretend to be, are you?" he taunted. "On the surface it's all frosty dignity, but underneath the fires are burning—I can feel their heat."

"No," she protested, desperately trying to twist free of him. "You're wrong..."

"Am I?" he challenged, drawing her closer against him, his arm sliding around her slender waist. "Then you won't let me kiss you, will you?"

She caught her breath on a small gasp of shock, putting up her hand against his chest—but any intention she might have had to push him away melted as she felt the warmth of hard muscle beneath his white silk shirt. He laughed in mocking contempt as he recognised her lack of resistance.

"Now you're showing yourself in your true colours," he taunted, his head bending over hers.

His mouth was firm and sensuous, inciting her to respond, and her lips parted tremblingly as with unhurried ease his languorous tongue sought the soft inner sweetness, plundering in a deliberately flagrant exploration of all the deep, secret corners within. She closed her eyes, her head tipping back into the crook of his arm, melting in a honeyed tide of submissiveness, drugged by the musky male scent of his skin. She had been aching for this from the moment she had first set eyes on him—it had been an instantaneous reaction, far beyond the reach of reason...

But she shouldn't be allowing it to happen... With a sudden rush of shame, she tried to pull back, but his hold on her hardened, his kiss becoming an insolent assault that she knew was intended to punish and humiliate. In a panic to get away from him, to deny the frightening power of her own desire, she deliberately sank her teeth into his lip.

"Bitch!" He let her go, anger flaring in his eyes. A small trickle of blood had appeared at the corner of his mouth, and she stared at it in horror.

"I . . . I'm . . . sorry. I didn't mean . . . to hurt you," she stammered, pain twisting in her heart. "But you . . . shouldn't have done that."

"No, I shouldn't," he conceded on a harsh note of anger. "You're the woman who stood at the altar with my cousin not more than a few hours ago, vowing to forsake all others. You didn't manage to keep it up for very long, did you?"

She drew in a long, deep breath, struggling to control the ragged beat of her heart. "Please don't ever touch me again," she insisted with fierce dignity. "I'm Jeremy's wife, and I intend to do everything I can to make him happy. I don't care whether you believe me or not—time will prove that I mean what I say."

And, turning him an aloof shoulder, she gathered up the rustling silk folds of her wedding-dress and hurried away, back through the quiet shadows of the garden to the safety of the bright, crowded marquee.

CHAPTER THREE

MADDY turned away from the window—but the guilty memory of that kiss still haunted her heart, as it had for almost nine years. She had known as she had run from the rose-walk that she had made a terrible mistake by marrying Jeremy—but as she had slipped back into the marquee he had spotted her, darting over to catch her up in his arms, and she had known that she couldn't tell him.

She had tried—she really had—to make him happy. Maybe if she hadn't got pregnant so quickly... But all too soon she had been suffering morning sickness that had lasted for most of the day, and then the discomfort of swollen ankles which had forced her to rest with her feet up for a good deal of the time.

She hadn't seen much of Leo; after his engagement to Saskia had ended he had gone back to America for almost a year, and even after his return they had met only at family gatherings, where he had never been more than distant and polite towards her—she could almost have believed that that kiss had been the product of her own fevered imagination.

Sometimes she had wondered if Jeremy sensed something, try as she might to hide it from him. Maybe that had been why things had started to go wrong...? But no—it had been his unwillingness to face up to the realities of life, to the constant demands of a small baby, to the need to spend money on boring things like repairs to the roof instead of a shiny new car.

And ultimately if had been finding one of Saskia's earrings on the back seat of his car, and his sheepish admission that he had been having an affair with her on and off for most of the time they had been married.

She had almost been expecting something of the kind, but that it had been Saskia had been the worst blow of all. Suddenly more than ten years of her own history seemed to have been cast into a different light, showing up all the glaring faults in that friendship that had been one of the few things she had had to hold on to. She had been able to forgive, but not to forget, and in the end they had agreed quite amicably that they couldn't go on.

And now she was going to have to deal with all those unresolved feelings that had lain dormant for so long. It had taken her about two seconds to realise that Leo still had the same devastating effect on her—and only a little longer to realise that he still regarded her with the same thinly veiled contempt.

The sound of voices downstairs in the hall warned her that Jeremy's sister had returned; she pulled a wry face, but she was going to have to face her sooner or later, so it might as well be now. Drawing in a long, steadying breath, she crossed the room and opened the bedroom door. At least she had the slight advantage of being the one descending the stairs—even when she had lived here, Julia had somehow always managed to make her feel as though she was an interloper in this house, that she had no right to be here. This time she was going to have to assert herself right from the beginning.

Jeremy's sister was only a few years older than herself, but her imperious manner had always made her appear much older. Her voice, as she handed out instructions to Mrs Harris about what to cook for dinner, had the quality of cut glass. Halfway down the stairs, Maddy paused for effect, armoured with a cool dignity that nine years ago she would have given anything to possess.

"Good afternoon, Julia," she greeted her, pleased to note that her voice was well under control.

The older woman glanced up, her expression registering a faint surprise. "Madeleine...!" She recovered herself quickly. "You managed to find the time to come over, then?" she enquired with stiff cordiality. "Is Jamie with you?"

Maddy refused to allow herself to be needled. "Yes, he's here—he's down in the kitchen, playing with his kitten." With a flicker of surprise, she recognised the two children who had arrived with her sister-in-law. "Goodness, it's...Aubrey and Venetia, isn't it? How you've grown!"

"It's a long time since you've seen them," Julia reminded her with a touch of asperity. "Run along downstairs, you two," she added briskly to the children. "And don't make a nuisance of yourselves."

Aubrey, the older of the two—he would be about ten now, by Maddy's reckoning—slanted his mother a look of cool insolence that would have earned Jamie a good smack, and with a small shrug of his shoulders which implied that his mother's injunction was insultingly juvenile for one of his mature years strolled away in the direction of the kitchen door. Venetia, meanwhile—a plain, dumpy child of the same age as Jamie—pouted and put her thumb in her mouth, clutching at her mother's skirt.

"Oh, for goodness' sake!" Julia exclaimed impatiently, brushing her off. "Don't be so clingy, child." She reached into her handbag and took out a bar of chocolate. "Here, take this and run along."

The child snatched the chocolate and ran off without even thinking of saying thank you. Maddy was a little startled, and glad that she had brought Jamie up better than that. But then Julia had never seemed to have much time for her children even when they were babies, happily leaving them with a nanny almost from the time they were born.

"Where's Leo?" Julia queried.

"In the library, I believe."

"Ah, good—I was hoping he'd still be here. Is your room satisfactory, by the way?"

"Yes, thank you," Maddy responded with careful restraint.

Julia smiled with her habitual air of condescension. "Of course. If you need anything, do ask the house-keeper. Now, if you'll excuse me, I have some important business to discuss with Leo..."

At that moment the door to the library opened, and Leo himself appeared. "Ah, Julia," he drawled, an inflection of sardonic humour in his voice. "I thought I heard your dulcet tones."

Julia's eyes flickered in momentary annoyance at being greeted with such a lack of respect, but she returned her cousin one of her tight little smiles. "There you are, Leo. I was just coming to look for you."

"So I gathered," he responded drily. "If the business you want to discuss is about the house, Maddy will have to be included. She's a co-trustee, you know."

Julia lifted one finely drawn eyebrow in well-bred surprise, but conceded with a small shrug of her shoulders. "Of course. Well, perhaps we'd better all go into the library," she suggested graciously, inviting Maddy to join them with a polite gesture of her hand.

Leo stood aside to let them pass, a glint of enigmatic amusement in those agate eyes. Maddy stepped past him warily; reliving those memories of their earlier encounters had made the intervening years seem to evaporate, making it feel as if it had all happened only yesterday. She could only hope that their meeting again had not had the same effect on him.

Julia swept through the door, glancing around with a proprietorial air. "Ah, this always was one of my favourite rooms," she remarked with satisfaction. "I always remember my father, sitting in that chair by the fireplace with his pipe and his newspaper..."

"You must have an awfully good memory, then," Leo responded on a note of lazy mockery. "He was rarely at home, and when he was he was hardly a pipe-and-slippers man."

She flashed him a look of icy disdain, and sat down in the best armchair, leaving Maddy to take the smaller one opposite her while Leo moved over to lean against the marble fireplace.

"So what did you want to discuss, Julia?" he enquired without preamble.

She smiled, an air of smugness about her that made Maddy watch her suspiciously. "I see you've begun trying to sort out poor Jeremy's financial affairs," she remarked. "I dare say it's all in a terrible muddle?"

"It's pretty confused," he acknowledged drily.

"There won't be a lot of money left, not with death duties to pay—I don't think he'd even finished paying off the last lot, from when Daddy died."

"I haven't come to that yet," Leo responded. "No doubt I shall find the papers sooner or later."

"And the state of the house! It's such a pity he's let it fall into such disrepair—it's going to cost a small fortune to put it right. No doubt you'll be thinking about selling it?''

"Possibly." he conceded. "It'll be a while before I can decide what will have to be done."

"You know it will have to be sold!" she rapped impatiently. "I've talked it over with Nigel, and he's prepared to make you a very good offer for it."

"Oh?" A faintly sardonic smile curved Leo's firm mouth. "You're very quick off the mark, Julia—I haven't even begun to consider what it might be worth."

"Well, naturally you'll want an independent valuation first," Julia acknowledged. "But I would hate to see it go outside the family. And I think I should have the right to first refusal..."

"No!" They both turned to Maddy, startled by her unexpected outburst. She was a little startled herself, but she spoke with absolute certainty. "The house isn't for sale. It belongs to Jamie."

Julia snorted with impatience. "Do be sensible, my dear. It would be simply impossible to keep it up on the kind of income the estate will be left with. If it's sold, and the money properly invested, it will be more than enough to keep you both very comfortably."

"I don't want to sell it," Maddy reiterated, her voice very controlled. She was having some difficulty keeping her anger in check; how dared they sit there and plan the disposal of her son's birthright, as if she had no say in the matter at all?

Leo was regarding her with that dark, level gaze she found so difficult to read. "And how, exactly, do you propose to raise the money to keep the place going?" he enquired.

"I... haven't quite settled that yet," she responded coolly; she needed a little more time to work out the figures and discuss them with her accountant before she revealed her hand—she wanted to present him with an absolutely water-tight business plan, one that even he would be able to find no fault with.

"Well, I don't think that's—" Julia broke off abruptly as the door burst open and her son catapulted into the room, his hand clamped to his left eye. "Aubrey! Whatever—?"

"He hit me!" the child wailed petulantly.

"Who hit you?" Julia demanded, gathering him to her bosom.

"Jamie did! He punched me and he kicked me."

"Oh, my poor darling...!" The indignant mother turned in fury on the smaller child hovering uncertainly in the doorway. "You nasty little bully," she scolded him furiously. "How dare you hit poor Aubrey? You'd better apologise this minute, or you'll be more than sorry!"

Maddy fired up instantly in defence of her own son. "Wait a minute," she protested. "Let's find out who started it first. Jamie, what happened?"

The small boy stood in the doorway with his fists clenched, an obdurate expression on his face. "Am not going to say sorry," he insisted.

"Jamie?" Maddy looked at him in surprise. Like any boy of his age he was inclined to get into the occasional playground scrap, but it never amounted to much and he was usually best friends with his opponent again almost as soon as they had picked themselves up. "Why did you hit Aubrey?" she asked him in her sternest voice.

He looked up at her, a world of hurt in his soft brown eyes, but she knew the set of that jaw—he could be as stubborn as his father at times. "Won't tell," he declared.

Maddy frowned. There was clearly something wrong, but she couldn't let him get away with defying her like this. "Jamie, if you hit Aubrey, that was very naughty of you—you know that. I don't care what he said to you—sticks and stones may break your bones but words can never hurt you. I want you to say you're sorry."

"No!" Abruptly he turned and fled, running up the stairs towards his bedroom.

Maddy moved to chase after him, but Leo's firm hand on her arm detained her. "Let me deal with him," he suggested quietly.

She glared up at him, furious at his intrusion—wasn't it enough for him to try to take over everything else, without interfering with the way she brought up her son? But swift second thoughts suggested that perhaps he was right—there was something in this situation that could be better handled by a man. So she held back, and let him go.

Julia was still cooing over the wailing Aubrey. "Look what he's done to him, the vicious little bully," she protested indignantly. "He's going to have the most dreadful black eye! There, there, darling, don't cry—here, have a nice piece of chocolate."

"Putting a steak on it will do more good," Maddy recommended tersely. "And as for Jamie being a bully, that's ridiculous—he's more than two years younger than Aubrey!"

It was almost an hour later, and Maddy was alone in the library going through some of Jeremy's papers, when Leo reappeared. She glanced up as he came into the room, closing the door behind him. "Is he all right?" she asked quickly.

He nodded, a wry smile curving that firm, well-shaped mouth. "Little tyke. That was a really good pop he got in on Aubrey, considering he's such a little feller."

"I hope you didn't tell him so!" she protested indignantly. "He doesn't need any encouragement to fight."

"No—he's just like Jeremy was at the same age," he mused reminiscently. "I was always dragging him out of trouble when he'd been mixing it with boys twice his size."

"Did you find out what it was all about?" she enquired.

"I did. But I promised him I wouldn't tell you."

"You promised what?" she demanded sharply. "How dare you? He's my son, in case you'd forgotten...!"

"I hadn't forgotten," he responded with a faint smile. "But there are some things that can only be dealt with between men—women wouldn't understand."

She glared at him in cold fury—but then to her surprise detected a glint of genuine amusement in his eyes.

"Let it go," he urged gently. "I'll smooth Julia's feathers. Forget it even happened."

She forced herself to draw in a long, steadying breath, and by the time she answered she had realised that he had a point. "All right," she conceded reluctantly. "But please don't think I'm giving you permission to get involved in my son's life on a regular basis. You may be a co-trustee, but I'm his sole guardian. We've got along perfectly well for the past five years by ourselves, thank you, and I have every confidence that we will continue to do so."

Rather to her surprise, he didn't argue. Moving across the room, he perched on the edge of the desk beside her, glancing down at the contents of the shoe-box she was going through. "Making any headway?" he enquired.

"A little," she responded, conscious of a slight tremor of nervousness in her voice; he was just a little too close, and she was just a little too aware of the latent power in that hard-muscled body, the faint musky scent of his skin. "I've... been trying to sort out which bills haven't been paid. There seem to be rather a lot of them."

"I'm afraid so," he concurred, apparently unaware of any tension in the air. "Have you looked at the surveyor's report for dealing with the dry rot in the cellar?"

"I have." She drew the paper towards her from the pile, frowning over it. "It'll have to be done—and soon. Otherwise it'll just get worse."

"Quite. Nor is that the only thing that's going to need attention within the near future—the central heating needs a drastic overhaul, and the drains are in urgent need of repair. The long-term problem is that the farm leases simply don't generate sufficient revenue to maintain the estate." He was watching her, an enigmatic glint in those amber-flecked eyes. "It really would be the most sensible thing to do—to sell the house."

She shook her head. "No—not without a fight," she asserted, her mouth set in a line as obstinate as Jamie's had been. "And you can't sell it without my agreement."

He lifted one dark eyebrow, as if faintly amused by her forceful determination. "I wouldn't dream of it," he responded, in a tone that made her suspect that he had already considered the option and discarded it. "And certainly not to Julia—I have no wish to see the place turned into a golf club."

Maddy glanced up at him in surprise. "A golf club?"

"That's what Nigel has in mind for it."

"Oh... But I thought... I got the impression Julia was intending to live here."

"I dare say she would," he remarked drily. "If she could afford it. Unfortunately even poor Nigel's purse wouldn't stretch to the mortgage they'd need to take on, let alone the cost of upkeep."

"Well, no, I suppose not," Maddy mused. "The only people who have that sort of money in their pockets these days are oil barons and pop stars, or—" She stopped abruptly, the realisation striking her that Leo himself could probably afford it—if he wanted to...

He seemed to read her mind. "Yes, I could buy it," he confirmed evenly. "If it was for sale."

"Which it isn't."

"We seem to have already established that," he acknowledged with a dry smile. "However, I have another suggestion—or perhaps it would be more accurate to call it a ... proposal."

Something odd in his voice made her glance up at him, frowning. "A proposal?"

"You want the house to pass to Jamie—but without a decent injection of cash it's unlikely that you'll be able to hold on to it," he pointed out coolly. "I have the cash. So I'm suggesting that you should marry me—after a decent interval of time, of course. We wouldn't want to shock the whole neighbourhood by an appearance of undue haste."

She stared up at him in blank shock. His voice, his manner, seemed quite normal... Maybe she had misheard him? "I'm ... sorry," she managed, her voice wavering. "What did you say?"

"I asked you to marry me," he responded, a flicker of sardonic amusement in those agate eyes. "I'm sorry—I've probably taken you rather by surprise. You'll need some time to consider, of course. Shall I ask Peggy to send us up some coffee?"

"C-coffee?"

"Or would you prefer something a little stronger? Brandy, perhaps?" He crossed the room to the antique mahogany chiffonier, and poured her a large tumbler of Jeremy's best cognac. "Do you want ginger with it, or do you prefer it straight?"

"Straight," she managed weakly—she needed it.

He smiled as he handed her the glass. "Good girl— it would be a crime to ruin a good cognac by adding fizzy pop."

She took it from him, taking a large gulp that scalded her throat. "I'm...afraid I don't quite understand," she said, struggling to match his sang-froid. "Why do you want to marry me?"

He had poured himself a brandy too, and sat down in one of the armchairs beside the fireplace, his long legs stretched out lazily across the hearth. "I've been considering getting married for a while now," he explained, his tone one of casual detachment. "I'm in my middle thirties, and frankly I'm becoming a little bored with a bachelor existence. I really don't have the time for all that romance and flattery routine you have to go through with every new woman you meet."

Maddy shot him a look of sharp comprehension. "To get them into bed, you mean?" she bit out acidly.

"Exactly," he conceded, unruffled. "Having a wife would be far more convenient."

"Oh, of course," she acknowledged, her voice shaking only slightly. "You could have sex on tap, as it were. But why me, in particular? There must surely be plenty of other candidates to choose from?"

"Possibly. Unfortunately, that would leave me no better off—most wives would expect me to dance attendance on them, to buy them flowers and remember their birthday. However, I believe that you and I could come to a mutually satisfactory agreement. You would be able to ensure that Jamie's inheritance remains safely intact, and in return you would be...available to me whenever I wanted you."

"I see." Only the hot glitter of her eyes betrayed the boiling cauldron of hurt and anger that was churning inside her. "In other words, you're offering me an elegant form of prostitution."

"If you choose to put it like that," he acknowledged evenly.

"It seems to be the only way to describe it. It's very flattering, of course, that you should think my...services are worth that much." Her jaw was aching with the effort of controlling the explosion that was building up inside her. "However, I would like to explore some other options first."

He lifted one dark eyebrow in polite interest. "Such as?"

She hesitated, reluctant to tell him of her plans prematurely. "I've...been considering ways to use the house itself to generate income," she explained cautiously. "Some of the downstairs rooms in the east wing would make a wonderful venue for parties, wedding receptions—that sort of thing. We're close enough to town to be convenient for guests, and it wouldn't involve turning the whole place over to it."

He appeared to give the suggestion some considered thought. "It could be feasible," he conceded. "But would it be enough to bring in the sort of money the house will need?"

"I'm not sure of that yet," she returned. "My idea is not just to hire the rooms out, but to offer a complete party service—all the arrangements, the food, entertainment... We could even capitalise on the ghost, and offer all-night ghost-watching parties!''

"Hmm. It sounds interesting,'' he acknowledged. "But it would involve a great deal of work. There'd be the catering, for a start, and you'd probably need to get a drinks licence—and even an entertainment licence.''

"I know. But I already have quite a bit of experience. I...don't know if Jeremy ever mentioned it to you, but since we split up I've been running a small business as a party planner—it's doing rather well. I think it would be quite easy to develop it, and I'm sure people would find it useful to be able to buy the whole package and not have to worry about any of the details at all.''

"I see.'' There was nothing in his manner that betrayed his feelings about her rejection of his proposal. "Do you have a business plan?''

"Not yet—I'm still formulating my ideas,'' she responded evenly. "I shall need to talk it over with my accountant, and of course it will be necessary to have some idea of how much money will have to be committed to urgent repairs to the house, and to paying the death duties. I would say I should be able to have something on paper within about two weeks. Of course,'' she added, regarding him with cold suspicion, "as co-trustee I would need your agreement.''

"Naturally.'' His smile was provocative. "And you're wondering whether I'll block your idea in order to force you to accept mine?''

"Will you?''

He shook his head. "That would just make you resent me, which wouldn't make life very comfortable for either of us. No, I support your plans—for an agreed period. Shall we say six months? And then if you find things aren't working out as well as you hope, we can discuss my offer again. Does that seem reasonable?''

Maddy drew in a long, steadying breath. It seemed reasonable—far too reasonable, too cold-blooded. But she had enough confidence in her own ability to make a success of her party scheme to be reasonably sure that it would never have to come to that—if he kept his word...

"Very well," she conceded warily. "I'll be prepared to discuss it."

"Good." He lifted his glass, toasting her, a mocking glint lurking in the depths of those agate eyes. "Shall we drink to it?"

She sipped her brandy, her eyes glittering beneath her lashes as she watched him. She didn't trust him, he was far too dangerous an opponent. And from what she knew of him, he usually won.

His proposal had been as unexpected as it was unwelcome. At least he had made it clear what the game was—she was just afraid that he was going to make up his own rules as he went along. But she wasn't going to let him know that it disturbed her—that would give him too much power. And she had a very uncomfortable feeling that he had far too much of that already.

Maddy had always found refuge in the kitchen quarters when Julia was in the house. Mrs Harris was cooking a Beef Wellington for dinner, and the smell was mouthwatering. "Can I give you a hand?" she enquired as the housekeeper bustled about, preparing vegetables.

"Oh, good heavens, no!" Mrs Harris looked scandalised. "Of course not!"

Maddy chuckled with laughter. "Why on earth not? I'm not some fine lady whose hands would drop off if

she dipped them in the washing-up water, you know—
I'm used to hard work. Here, let me peel the potatoes
while you get on with the soup.''

"Don't you want to go up and get changed for
dinner?'' Mrs Harris protested.

Maddy shook her head. "I'm not going to bother,''
she asserted with a hint of defiance. "I'm afraid if they
don't like me sitting down in my jeans, they can lump
it.''

Mrs Harris grinned at her in wry amusement, knowing
very well that Julia wouldn't like it at all. "It's your
house,'' she encouraged her gently.

"Well, no, it's Jamie's house, to be precise,'' Maddy
amended with a smile. "But it isn't Julia's house—and
it never will be.''

Mrs Harris nodded in grim satisfaction. "Beats me
why she's suddenly so dead set on the old place anyway.
Time was she couldn't wait to get away from it—used
to call it an old dump.''

"Well, yes—but I expect when she was younger it must
have seemed like that to her,'' Maddy mused, trying to
be fair. "It isn't until you get a little older that you really
learn to appreciate good things. For a kid of Jamie's age
all the grounds must seem like a paradise to play in, but
I don't suppose he'll really value the house for quite a
few years yet.''

"Oh, I don't know,'' Mrs Harris chuckled. "He wasn't
slow to put young Aubrey in his place earlier on.''

Maddy glanced at her in surprise. "What do you
mean?'' she queried, frowning.

"That's what they were fighting about,'' Mrs Harris
told her. "Aubrey was trying to shove the lad away from
where he was playing on the floor with that kitten of
his. So young Jamie flares up at him, telling him as how

it was his house, and he could play wherever he wanted.
Then Aubrey says that if it weren't for you, the house
would have been his mother's instead. So Jamie hit
him—a really good one, right in the eye—and the big
girl's blouse goes off crying to his mother."

"I see . . ." Maddy couldn't help but be impressed that
her son had already developed such a fierce pride in his
inheritance. Not that she liked him fighting over it—but
it seemed that Mrs Harris was as ready to excuse him
for that as Leo had been.

"Mind, it's his mother I blame—for teaching him to
say things like that," the housekeeper asserted, her
mouth a grim line. "Where else would he have got it
from, if not from her? And the plain fact is if poor Mr
Jeremy had still been here they wouldn't have had the
house anyway, and talk like that makes it sound as if
they were wishing him gone so they could get their hands
on it."

"Oh, no—I'm sure it's nothing like that," Maddy
protested quickly. "I suppose it's just understandable
that they'd see me as an outsider, and resent that."

"You're certainly not an outsider," Mrs Harris protested. "You took more care of this place while you was
here than either Mr Jeremy or his father ever did—God
rest 'em both. And it couldn't be in better hands now.
I said to my Sara—you remember, that's my youngest;
she works in the hairdressers in the village now—I said
to her this morning, as soon as I heard you was coming
down, You wait, we'll see that pointing fixed on the east
chimney now, before another storm fetches it down."

"Of course," Maddy murmured, adding yet another
urgent repair to her mental list, and wondering to herself
how much that one was likely to cost. Mrs Harris clearly

had very high expectations of her, she reflected wryly—she only hoped she would be able to live up to them...

They both glanced up in some surprise as the door opened and Julia appeared. She shot Maddy a glance of speaking disapproval—it was really not quite done to linger down here, chatting to the servants—and turned to the housekeeper.

"Ah, Mrs Harris—I just popped down to let you know that there'll be one extra for dinner. My sister-in-law has come over. Maddy, don't you want to change?" she added pointedly. "We're dining early, as the children will be eating with us."

"Oh, I thought we'd be informal," Maddy responded, the note of assurance in her voice calculated as a reminder that she was the hostess, not Julia. "I'm sure no one will bother with what we're all wearing, under the circumstances."

The other woman's eyes flashed coldly. "As you please," she conceded tautly, and, turning on her heel, she walked out, closing the door behind her with a firm click.

Maddy sighed. She hadn't enjoyed being forced into a clash of wills with Julia—they should rather be united in grief at the moment. But she knew that if she didn't assert herself now it would only get worse—Julia was perfectly capable of moving in and taking over as if she really did own the place!

And the information that Saskia had arrived wasn't entirely welcome, either. She hadn't seen her for almost six years—not since she had left Jeremy. What was she supposed to say to her? Unfortunately there were no guidelines on the etiquette to be followed when meeting your late husband's mistress. It promised to be a difficult evening.

"I think perhaps I will change out of these jeans, after all," she mused, her voice carefully casual. "It wouldn't hurt just to slip into a dress."

CHAPTER FOUR

HALF an hour later, Maddy was glad that she had decided to change into a slightly more formal outfit. She always felt more confident when she knew she was well-groomed, and her slimly tailored dress of French navy blue, neatly belted around her slender waist, created exactly the image of dignity and composure she wished to convey. Pausing briefly to check her reflection in the mirror one last time, tucking a wayward strand of her wheat-coloured hair back into place, she closed her bedroom door behind her and slipped along the corridor to her son's room.

"Jamie? Come along, put that computer game away now," she insisted gently. "It's time to go to down to dinner."

"Oh, Mum!" he protested, not lifting his head from the hand-held game he was playing with.

"Dinner!" she reiterated. "You can play with it again afterwards—but not for more than half an hour, mind."

"But Uncle Leo gave it to me," he argued, as if that ought to be the clincher.

"Not to make you late for dinner," she asserted. "*Now*, young man—or I shan't let you play with it at all tomorrow. And have you washed your hands?"

Reluctantly the child relinquished the game, giving her a look as if she was the cruellest tyrant since Stalin. "Just going to," he temporised, trailing over to the sink in the corner.

She smiled down at that soft brown head, obstinately averted as he walked past her. He was so like his father in so many ways—hating to be thwarted. But fortunately he lacked Jeremy's casual selfishness—he would go out of his way to avoid upsetting anyone.

His sunny personality was quickly restored as he danced beside her down the stairs. "I got my highest score ever," he announced proudly. "Four thousand, three hundred and twenty-five."

"Well done," she approved. "You must be almost the champion!"

"Not yet," he acknowledged modestly. "But Uncle Leo says that if I keep practising I can only get better."

"Oh, did he?" Maddy responded, mentally noting the intention to have a few words with Leo about encouraging her son to spend all his time playing computer games.

They had reached the half-landing above the wide hall when the door of the drawing-room opened and Saskia appeared. She glanced up, as startled as Maddy by this premature encounter, and for a long, tense moment the two of them stared at each other, neither of them quite sure how to react.

Maddy realised with some surprise that she had forgotten how tiny Saskia was—a dainty, frail, vulnerable creature, her pale blonde hair emphasised by a dress of unrelieved black, high-necked and long-sleeved, almost Victorian in its proclamation of sombre mourning.

The years, and two brief and disappointing marriages, had changed her little, Maddy mused—she still wore her hair in the same fringe, she still favoured pearl-pink lipstick and pale blue eyeshadow. It was rather a dated look now, and perhaps didn't quite do her justice.

And then, as she hesitated, the other girl came towards her, both hands warmly outstretched. "Maddy! It's been so long...! Oh, and you've cut off all your lovely hair—what a pity." Artlessly she put up one hand to toss her own long, pale, silken locks back over her shoulder—a gesture that Maddy now knew well enough to guess was really not artless at all.

What game was she playing? She was quite sure that Saskia must know that she had been aware of what had been going on between her and Jeremy, but there she was acting as guiltless as a newborn babe, the long-lost best friend—and with Jamie at her side, quicker than lightning to pick up anything odd and certain to ask awkward questions about it, she had little choice but to go along with the pretence.

"Hello, Sass," she responded, managing some kind of smile as she walked on down the stairs—though she didn't go so far as to take the other girl's hands. "It certainly has been a long time—though you haven't changed a bit."

"Nor have you! My goodness, we've so much to catch up on! Though...it's so sad that it had to take something like this to bring us back together," she added, dabbing the screwed up handkerchief she was clutching to the corner of her eye—though taking care not to smudge her mascara, Maddy couldn't help but notice. "Poor Jeremy. I still can't quite believe it!"

Maddy smiled a little crookedly. In spite of the breathless delivery, there was no doubt that Saskia was genuinely deeply upset—all the more shocked, perhaps, because in her sheltered, privileged life she had so rarely had to face up to any harsh realities. "I know," she agreed, laying a gentle hand on the other girl's shoulder. "It was a terrible shock."

"I... do hope that at least you and I can be friends again now," Saskia appealed wistfully. "It made me so sad that just because you'd split up with Jeremy you felt you had to stop speaking to me as well." Those blue eyes were as accusing as a whipped puppy's. "I thought you were my best friend."

Maddy stared at her, lost for words. How could she...? But at that moment Leo came out into the hall, and to her surprise she felt her heart give an odd little thump; again, there were no simple rules of social behaviour to guide how one should behave towards a man whose proposal of marriage one had just turned down—particularly when the proposal had been made with such ruthless cold-bloodedness.

Jamie bounced over to him immediately. "Hi, Uncle Leo! Guess what? I beat my last score by almost five hundred!"

Leo smiled down at him, ruffling his soft brown hair carelessly with one hand. "Really? That's very good. I hope you haven't been forgetting everything else while you've been playing it, though?"

Jamie looked a tad sheepish, and slanted a swift glance up at Maddy, pleading with her not to tell. She shot Leo a glittering glare, inconsistently annoyed that now he should be scolding Jamie for spending too much time playing with the toy, when only moments ago she had been annoyed that he was encouraging him. It was not his place to tell her son what to do...

Goodness—she was actually jealous, she realised with a sharp stab of self-awareness; Leo's good opinion, it seemed, was more important to her son than anything else. She really ought to be grateful for that, she chided herself sternly—the boy needed a father-figure, and it would be very unfair to let her own feelings damage the relationship between them.

"He only plays when I tell him he can," she answered a little stiffly. "He's very good about it."

"You've been playing EcoWarrior?" Saskia jumped in with a bright smile—which was a little odd since she seemed to have had no interest at all in Jamie until Leo had joined them. "You must show me—I keep asking Leo, but he says he doesn't have time." She lifted an admonishing blue gaze to the man at her side, pouting prettily. "I'm afraid I'm not very quick at learning that sort of thing—it all seems so complicated to me."

Maddy felt her teeth go on edge; surely at the age of twenty-nine Saskia should have outgrown that sort of girlish sweetness by now? And surely it must be wasted on a man of Leo's intelligence? But there was no guarantee of that, she reflected acidly—men could be just plain stupid when some simpering miss gave them the "You Tarzan, me Jane" act.

The brief gathering was interrupted by Julia, swanning out from the drawing-room. "Ah, there you are Madeleine," she remarked with one of her light little smiles, a discreet glance at her watch suggesting that Maddy had been keeping them waiting. "Shall we go in to dinner? We don't want it to get cold."

"Oh, we don't need to worry about that," her husband declared cheerfully, following her out into the hall. "It's Mrs H's splendid cold cucumber soup—it won't matter if we leave it standing another half an hour! Well, Maddy! How-de-do?" he added, greeting her with a slightly less than avuncular kiss on the cheek. "It's good to see you again—and still as beautiful as ever! Young Jeremy was a lucky dog—often told him so...!"

"Nigel." Julia summoned his attention imperiously. "We're going in to dinner."

He rolled his eyes in an exaggerated impersonation of a small boy caught with a spoon in the honey-pot, and obediently moved to his wife's side. Maddy ignored Julia's fulminating glare—surely she didn't seriously think that she would have encouraged her husband's smarmy advances? But Julia was capable of believing anything; she would have thought Leo more astute, however, but he too was frowning in disapproval. Well, let him think what he damned well liked, she asserted fiercely to herself, and, turning him an aloof shoulder, she followed the others into the dining-room.

Julia moved towards the head of the table, but then hesitated pointedly. "Of course, you'll wish to sit at the head of the table, won't you, Madeleine?" she enquired with an exaggerated show of deference. "I wouldn't wish you to think I was trying to usurp your place."

"Thank you," Maddy countered in saccharine tones; she was in a Catch-22 situation, she reflected with a touch of acid amusement—if she let Julia take the seat she would give her the satisfaction of continuing to play the lady of the manor, but by taking it herself she made herself appear pettily concerned about such trivial matters of precedence.

But it seemed that she was already regarded as the arch-villainess around here, so there was little point in worrying about it—there was nothing she could do to change their minds. And she really didn't care what they thought of her, anyway—least of all Leo. In fact, the more he disliked her, the less likely he was to pursue that crazy idea of marrying her.

Dinner was every bit as strained as she had antici-pated. Saskia had managed to wangle herself into the seat beside Leo, and was engaging him in a soft-voiced conversation that held his exclusive attention, while Julia had embarked on a lengthy enumeration of all the repairs needed on the house, together with a gloomy estimate of their cost and the possible consequences of delay in dealing with them.

"If it's as bad as that, I'm surprised you want to take it on yourself," Maddy was goaded into remarking.

"Ah, well... Sometimes you just can't help letting your heart rule your head," Julia responded with a heavy sigh. "I suppose when you've grown up somewhere it will always seem like home, no matter what."

Maddy winced, her hand creeping to the golden locket around her throat in an unconscious gesture of insecurity. She could understand Julia's feelings; after all, she loved the house although she had lived in it for little more than three years—she could imagine that for someone who had grown up here it would exert an even stronger influence.

And what about Leo? She slanted him a covert look from beneath her lashes, studying the arrogant lines of that hard-boned face. What did he feel about the house? He had grown up here too—at least since he was fifteen, when his father had died and he had come to live with Jeremy's parents. Did he share that same fierce possessiveness?

A small shiver ran through her. Was that why he had asked her to marry him? Was he planning to pressure her in some way to make over the house to him? If that was the case, it could be difficult to fight him—there was a streak of ruthlessness in him that she suspected always got him whatever he wanted.

And there was one area in which she was particularly vulnerable to him, she acknowledged ruefully; he had kissed her only once, a long time ago, but she had never been able to blot the memory of it from her mind. If he were to suspect that he had that sort of power over her she had no doubt that he wouldn't hesitate to use it against her. She was going to have to be very careful to ensure that she gave him no clue.

"Goodnight, sleep tight, mind the bed-bugs don't bite." Maddy bent to drop a light kiss on her son's forehead. "And don't play with that thing for more than half an hour. Promise?"

"I promise," he conceded, earnest brown eyes lifted to hers. "Mummy, do I have to show Auntie Saskia how to play it?"

Maddy laughed gently, stroking his soft brown hair. "I think you'll probably find she'll have forgotten all about it by now," she assured him.

He smiled in relief, and settled down against the pillow, the little black kitten tucked in beside him. Before Maddy had reached the door his head was bent in concentration over the shapes jogging across the small screen, the tip of his tongue showing between his teeth as he began zapping them out of existence.

Maddy slipped from the room and closed the door quietly behind her, a soft smile curving her mouth. He would almost certainly forget the time, and she would have to pop back upstairs later to remind him to put it away and go to sleep.

The corridor was in shadow, lit only by the light at the top of the stairs. Automatically she glanced up to check the smoke-alarm that she had insisted should be installed when she had first come to live here. The plastic cover was broken, hanging loose, but she could see there was still a battery in it. Quickly she fetched a chair from her own bedroom, and, perching on it, she reached up to test that the alarm was still working.

To her satisfaction a shrill siren pierced the quiet darkness. At once doors flew open upstairs and downstairs, startled faces stared at her. "What on earth was that?" Julia demanded indignantly.

"I was just making sure the smoke-alarm was working," she explained. "It's all right, Jamie, you can go back to bed—it was just a test this time."

Julia snorted in disgust. "You might have warned us," she protested. "That thing would wake the dead!"

"That's what it's supposed to do," Maddy responded pointedly, frowning as she tried to see why the plastic cover wouldn't click back properly into place.

Leo had come upstairs as soon as the alarm had sounded, and as she fiddled with the catch he came to see what she was doing. "What's wrong?" he enquired.

"It's broken," she informed him crisply. "It will have to be replaced. Hadn't you noticed it? It was hanging loose."

"No, I'm afraid I hadn't," he conceded. "Here, let me have a look at it."

He offered her his hand to step down from the chair. For a brief moment she hesitated, reluctant to accept even that fleeting touch. But on the other hand she didn't want him to know that it disturbed her in the least, so she took the proffered clasp briefly as she skipped to the ground, drawing her fingers swiftly away before it could have any effect.

He climbed up on to the chair and examined the alarm closely. "One of the hinges is broken. It'll do well enough for now, but we can get a new one tomorrow. Would you like me to help you check the rest of them?"

"I...I can manage," she insisted, reluctant to have him accompany her around the darkened house.

"Oh, I think I'd better come with you," he asserted, a glint of knowing amusement in his eyes. "You won't be able to reach all of them, even standing on a chair."

She knew that he was right—and she knew that she wouldn't be able to sleep until she had checked that every alarm in the house was working properly. It was a thought that always lurked in the back of her mind—if her parents had only had one fitted... So with a taut little nod she conceded.

The tour took some time. It was a rambling old building, and there were alarms in every corridor and in most of the rooms. They worked methodically from the attics to the basement, ending up in what had once been the butler's pantry and was now used as a dump for old bits of broken furniture that should have been thrown away.

"There. Happy now?" Leo enquired as the echoes of the last shrill siren bounced around the stone walls and faded away.

"Yes, thank you," she responded crisply. "But they ought to be checked every month, in case the batteries go flat."

"I usually do check them when I'm here," he told her. "It's a bit of a waste of time having the things if you don't bother to make sure they're working."

She nodded, swiftly stepping back as he climbed down from the chair, her heart fluttering in sudden agitation as she realised how close he was in the dimly lit basement room. A flicker of sardonic humour, that in anyone else would have been a smile, crossed his hard mouth.

"What's wrong?" he enquired mockingly.

"Nothing! I... We'd better be getting back upstairs..."

One dark eyebrow lifted in provocative question. "You're concerned that Julia might be worried about us?"

"Not Julia, no," she countered, unable to keep the caustic note from her voice. "But Saskia might start to wonder where we've got to."

"Oh?" The fleeting glint of anger in his eyes was disconcerting. "What makes you think that?"

She shrugged her slender shoulders in a speaking gesture. "Oh, nothing—it was just that the two of you seemed awfully tied up with each other this evening," she responded tautly.

"We're still friends," he grated. "Is there anything wrong with that?"

"Oh, really?" The conversation was drifting into dangerous waters, but Maddy wasn't sure how to re-direct it. "Don't tell me you haven't noticed the way she looks at you, with those great big blue eyes. She'd like to get her claws into you again."

"Don't be ridiculous!" he snapped impatiently. "Naturally Saskia is still very upset about Jeremy—the two of them were very close."

Maddy felt herself tense; if only he knew how close! But there was no point in even trying to tell him the truth now—it was too late for it to put anything right. Instead she gave another small shrug, turning towards the door. "Well, you can't blame me for wondering," she remarked lightly. "After all, it was only this afternoon that you were asking me to marry you."

"So I was," he murmured, a sardonic inflexion in his voice. With a small step sideways, he was blocking her retreat. "And you turned me down. Perhaps I was turning to Sass to soothe my hurt feelings."

"You don't have any feelings," she snapped in acid retort.

He laughed softly. "Oh, but I do," he argued, his voice taking on a huskier timbre. "In fact, they're stirring right now..."

"That isn't the sort of feeling I meant," she protested, taking a wary step back from him.

"Isn't it?" he taunted. "And yet you're feeling exactly the same. Don't try to deny it—it isn't just the darkness down here that's making the pupils of your eyes so large, and you haven't been running to make your breathing so ragged."

She stared up at him helplessly, unable to deny the betraying clues he had detected so easily, unable to escape as he put out his hand and stroked it along the smooth line of her jaw and round into her hair, holding her prisoner as he moved closer. A small quiver of electric charge shivered through her taut-strung nerve-fibres, and her lips parted instinctively as his head bent towards her.

It had been so long... She didn't know how to fight the treacherous tide of longing that was flowing through her. As he drew her against him she couldn't resist, her slender body moulding itself to the hard length of his, yielding to the strength of his embrace as he forced her to a shocking awareness of the full measure of his arousal.

His mouth was moving over hers, warm and enticing, his sensuous tongue plundering the depths within, inciting her to respond. With every breath the subtle musky scent of his skin was drugging her mind; she knew she ought not to be giving in to this dangerous temptation, but the forces inside her were way beyond her control...

He lifted his head at last, his eyes mocking as they gazed down into hers, his strong arms still locked around

her, refusing to let her go. "You see?" he growled. "If
I wanted to, I could take you right now."

She shook her head in desperate denial, her eyes wide
with panic. "No...!"

"Do you want me to prove it?" he challenged.

"No..." But she was weakening, the aching physical
need inside her stronger than her will to resist.

"Then admit it. Admit you want me."

She tipped back her head, straining away from him,
desperate to deny his words, but he still held her hard
against him, and the only effect of her struggles was to
crush her tender breasts against the hard wall of his chest,
and to mould her stomach and thighs into him with a
devastating intimacy that made her all too vividly aware
of the fierce tension of arousal in him.

"Admit it," he grated, his hand sliding up to mould
her ripe, aching breast, the pad of his thumb stroking
with a treacherous rhythm over the hardened, sensitised
nub of her nipple. "You want me to make love to you—
you have from the very first time we met. Even the day
you married Jeremy you were already being unfaithful
to him in your mind."

"I wasn't!" she protested, shaking her head. "I was
never unfaithful to him. It was—"

"What?" he demanded as she cut herself off abruptly. "What was it?"

With a bitter little stab of irony she remembered the
reasons why she couldn't tell him; more than ever now,
he would simply refuse to believe her. She had no choice
but to let him go on thinking the worst of her.
"It...wasn't like that," she insisted weakly. "I was never
unfaithful to him." But in the most essential sense he
was right, she acknowledged, the guilt searing her soul;
from the moment she had set eyes on Leo she had been

caught in some kind of evil spell, unable to exorcise the thought of him from her mind.

"No? Then what *was* it like?" he enquired with chilling sarcasm. "Or can't you bring yourself to admit it? You were out to trap any man who seemed to have enough money to keep you in the style to which you wished to become accustomed. When you realised I wasn't available, you turned your sights pretty smartly on poor Jerry, didn't you?"

"If you thought that, why didn't you tell him so?" she countered, icily furious.

"Oh, I tried. But the poor young fool was absolutely besotted with you. It was the first time in his life he ever got angry with me—he even accused me of wanting you for myself," he added with a bitter laugh.

"Well, maybe that wasn't so far from the truth," she countered acidly. "You didn't wait very long after he died to propose to me, did you?"

His eyes glinted with hard anger. "You really know how to hit below the belt, don't you?" he snarled, his hands sliding up to grasp her shoulders. "Yes, I want you. But let me warn you of one thing—you're not dealing with my cousin now. You played your little games with him—winding him round your dainty little finger, luring him on with promises that you had no intention of fulfilling—until you got exactly what you wanted. Well, you won't get away with that with me—our relationship is going to be strictly on my terms. I know just how to make you burn."

Holding her prisoner with that mesmerising gaze, he trailed one light fingertip along the line of her jaw and down the slender column of her throat, to linger in the soft shadow between her breasts. She drew in a sharp breath, shivering with the helpless panic of a small animal trapped by a very dangerous predator.

"It gave me no satisfaction to be proved right—to have to stand by and watch my cousin's marriage slide into inevitable disaster. This time around, you'll learn to take your vows more seriously."

"I'm...not going to marry you," she asserted raggedly. "I'm not going to be used just for your convenience. There's more to marriage than that."

"Is there?" he queried, his voice cool and soft. "Well, you should be the expert on that one, of course. But I think you'll find you won't have much choice but to change your mind—I very much doubt if you'll find this business scheme of yours will make enough money for you to keep the house. Sooner or later you'll be faced with either selling it, or selling yourself. And, believe me, if I buy, I shall expect to get my money's worth," he added, letting his gaze slide slowly down over her in an insolently detailed appraisal, lingering over every curve. "Every last penny's worth."

And on that note of chilling warning he turned and walked out of the room, leaving Maddy trembling in shocked reaction.

She sat down weakly on a nearby chair, which rocked alarmingly on a broken leg. She steadied it, balancing it on its remaining three good legs so that it wouldn't fall over. But it wasn't so easy to regain her own equilibrium. That had been exactly the kind of encounter she had known she should avoid—and the outcome had been exactly as she had feared; he knew all her weaknesses, knew exactly how to exploit them, and wouldn't scruple to do so at every opportunity.

And the really unnerving thing was that she was all too afraid that he was right; it was going to prove very

difficult indeed to make enough money to avoid the
spectre of being forced to make the choice he had outlined to her—to sell the house, or to accept his proposal.
At the moment, she wasn't sure which would be the
most unwelcome.

CHAPTER FIVE

THE funeral was held on Monday—precisely as Leo had decreed. A soft grey drizzle fell throughout the quiet service at the graveside—it seemed more appropriate, somehow, than sunshine. The whole Ratcliffe clan were out in force—cousins, aunts, distant relatives that Maddy had met only at her wedding and at Jamie's christening—as well as dozens of Jeremy's friends.

If she had thought those previous occasions a strain, they were nothing compared to this. She couldn't help but be aware that they were all watching her, with varying degrees of curiosity and hostility; if she cried some would accuse her of crocodile tears, while if she didn't others would accuse her of being heartless.

In the end it didn't matter what anyone thought of her—she couldn't help but shed a few quiet tears as the gleaming rosewood coffin was laid to rest. Jamie stood bravely at her side, clinging to her hand, and from time to time she squeezed his fingers for comfort, smiling down reassuringly into his bleak little face.

Leo stood on his other side. In spite of everything, Maddy would have liked nothing better than to have been able to lean on the support of those strong arms, but Saskia had appropriated their protection for herself, soaking his jacket as she wept copious tears.

The service came to an end, and one by one people began to drift away to the waiting line of cars. A few of them nodded to Maddy as they passed, and one or two even stopped to speak, but mostly they stepped rather awkwardly around the other way, to avoid the embarrassment of having to decide whether to acknowledge her or not.

She would have liked to have been the last to go—to have had a few moments alone to whisper a final goodbye—but it was more than apparent that Saskia intended to outstay her. She had turned into Leo's arms now, and was sobbing loudly, refusing to move away. So reluctantly Maddy stepped back, exchanged a few murmured words with the vicar—who had conducted her marriage as well—and with her arm lightly around her son's shoulders walked back to the car.

She was obliged to share the ride back to the house with Julia and Nigel, but fortunately it was only a short distance. She had insisted on bringing in extra help with preparing the food, so that Mrs Harris could attend the funeral, which gave her an excuse to slip away briefly as soon as they arrived, to check that everything was ready.

A cold buffet had been set out in the breakfast-room, and the wide double doors that linked it to the morning-room had been thrown open to allow plenty of space. It had stopped raining, and the pale winter sun was struggling to appear. Finding that there was nothing for her to do, Maddy wandered out through the French windows into the garden.

The signs of neglect were all too apparent out here. The roses hadn't been pruned properly for several years, and were looking leggy and sparse, and an ivy had been allowed to run rampant through the wistaria, almost choking it. Needing a few moments of quiet before she had to go back inside and face the throng, she strolled down through the bedraggled rose-walk.

Was it really so many years since she had walked here on her wedding-day? The old wooden seat was broken now, and weeds had grown up through the cobbled path; a little like her own life, she reflected wistfully—battered by the storms of bitter experience and the relentless cruelty of time.

The acid sting of tears pricked her eyes, and she tried to blink them back. She had never let herself dwell on "if only", but today she couldn't help it. If only she had never met Leo, maybe she would never have felt any reservations about her love for Jeremy—and then maybe everything would have been all right between them. Or if Leo hadn't been engaged to Saskia the first time she had met him...

"Maddy...?" Saskia's lightweight voice cut across her thoughts. "I'm glad I've found you. I...wanted to talk."

She turned, regarding her one-time friend with wry suspicion. "Oh? What about?"

Saskia came closer, smiling tentatively—her eyes, in spite of her noisy weeping at the churchyard, were remarkably clear. "It's been such a long time. Have you been keeping well?" she asked.

"Pretty well," Maddy responded briskly. "What about you?"

Mascaraed lashes swept down over rouged cheeks. "Oh, well... Things haven't turned out all that well for me, really. You know I got divorced again? I just don't seem to be very lucky when it comes to men—I always pick the wrong ones. I wish I could be more like you."

Maddy regarded her in some surprise. "Like me...?"

Saskia smiled up at her wistfully. "Well, at least you've got Jamie. I've always wanted children."

"Have you?" Maddy responded with a touch of asperity. "I don't remember it that way."

Those big blue eyes widened in astonishment. "How can you say that?" she protested. "I love children—I always have. You must remember—I always used to say I wanted a really big family."

Maddy shrugged; it probably wasn't worth arguing about—Saskia had never been the most consistent of people.

"It was Paul that didn't want children," Saskia went on sadly. "I think that was the main reason we split up. We used to argue about it all the time."

"What about your second husband?" Maddy enquired ingenuously.

"Oh, well . . ." Saskia's eyes slid away from hers, and she gave a strained little laugh. "That didn't really last long enough—we were only married six months. But still, I haven't given up hope," she added, brightening. "Third time lucky, you know?"

"Oh . . . ?"

The other girl giggled coyly. "I know you'll say I'm just a hopeless romantic, but . . . Well, since my divorce, Leo and I have been seeing quite a lot of each other, and . . . this time I honestly think we could make a go of it. We had something very special, you know, even though things didn't quite work out before."

Maddy had to hide her reaction swiftly. She wasn't exactly surprised—it had been obvious from the beginning that Saskia was keen to be a good deal more than friends with Leo. But her optimism that something could come of it seemed to suggest that he had given her some reason to believe that he felt the same.

So should she tell Saskia that he had proposed to her? Given what he had said about the matter, it seemed a little unfair to let her go on hoping in vain... But then Saskia was unlikely to welcome the information, even if she believed her, and besides, it wasn't really any of her business.

Saskia was looking up at her, an uncertain expression in those misty blue eyes. "I...wanted to say...I know you knew—about...me and Jeremy. I just wanted you to understand that...I never meant to break up your marriage. It was just one of those things that kind of...happened. We couldn't help it."

"Couldn't you?" Maddy queried, unable to keep the trace of bitterness from her voice.

Saskia pouted. "Well, I did know him long before you did," she argued, as if that made any difference.

"Yes, you did," Maddy agreed tautly. "But if you were so keen on him why didn't you marry him after I left him? I'd have given him a divorce if he'd asked me— he knew that."

Saskia looked faintly incredulous. "Marry Jerry? Oh, no, I never wanted to *marry* him. I mean, he was lots of fun to be with, and all that, but that's not enough, is it? I mean, if I was going to marry someone, they'd have to be...to be able to take care of me properly."

"They'd have to be rich, you mean?" Maddy returned caustically.

Saskia's mouth opened and closed like a fish as she struggled to deny what they both knew to be the truth. Any sympathy that Maddy had begun to feel for her evaporated.

"Look, Sass, it's a waste of time pretending that you and I can ever be friends again," she stated flatly. "Though to avoid any unpleasant speculation I'm prepared to put on a front. But that's as far as it goes."

The other girl returned her a look of glittering resentment, but then conceded with a small shrug. "All right—if that's the way you want it. But... there is just one little thing," she added, a wheedling note creeping into her voice. "You won't... tell Leo about Jerry and me, will you? He never knew about it, and... well..."

"No, I won't tell him," Maddy assured her coldly. "But not for your sake, nor for his—I'll keep the secret for Jeremy's sake. That's all." And, turning on her heel, she walked swiftly away—almost to collide with Leo as he stepped out through the French windows.

"Ah, there you are..." He looked past her to where Saskia stood, a picture of pathos, dabbing at her eyes with a screwed up handkerchief. "What's wrong?" he demanded of Maddy, a note of accusation in his voice.

"Nothing!" Maddy responded, her jaw taut with the effort of keeping her feelings under control. "We were just... reminiscing about old times." She didn't stop to explain any further, leaving Saskia to pour out any sneaking lies she liked into his ears. She didn't care—in fact she'd be delighted if the other girl succeeded in winning him back. The two of them deserved each other!

To Maddy's relief, quite a number of the family and old acquaintances seemed to have decided to be friendly towards her after all; it was Jamie who had broken the ice.

"What a charming little boy!" Great-Aunt Lucia remarked, smiling benignly down on him as he brought her a fresh glass of sherry. "So like his dear father."

"Yes, he is," Maddy agreed a little wistfully. "He has his eyes."

"You know, you're right!" the old besom declared. "And such charming manners. He's a credit to you, my dear."

"Thank you," Maddy murmured. She was looking for a discreet escape when Lucia's brother, Great-Uncle Henry, accosted her, hugging her shoulders in jovial familiarity.

"So, how are you coping?" he demanded. "Dare say the boy's left you nothing but debts. And then of course there'll be the death duties—terrible imposition! Still, you've got Leo to help you sort it all out—I'd just leave it all to him, if I were you. You don't want to go worrying your pretty little head with all that nonsense."

A soft laugh behind her made her stiffen. "I'm afraid Maddy wouldn't agree with you, Uncle Henry," Leo advised with a hint of lazy mockery. "She's got an...independent streak—she already has a few ideas buzzing for turning the old place into a profit-making enterprise."

The elderly gentleman looked a little alarmed. "Good heavens! You're not planning one of these damned safari parks, are you?"

"No, of course not!" she reassured him swiftly, casting Leo a jaundiced glare. "It's nothing that would change the character of the place at all."

"Hmm... Well..." He seemed only a little mollified. "I suppose if Leo approves of it..."

Maddy's eyes flashed, but before she could blurt out some unconsidered response Leo intervened smoothly. "I don't think you need to worry, Uncle Henry—I'm sure anything Maddy plans would be in good taste. Now, if you'll excuse us, there are one or two things we need to discuss." And, putting a hand beneath her elbow, he steered her gently but very firmly away.

She had to draw in a deep, steadying breath, more unsettled by his touch than she cared to admit. But she couldn't shake him off, not until they were in the library, safely away from any prying eyes. Then she took great satisfaction in dragging her arm very pointedly out of his grasp.

"There was something you wanted to discuss?" she queried crisply, moving across the room.

"Yes." His voice was terse to the point of annoyance. "For a start, there's no need for you to go upsetting Saskia. I don't know what stupid little thing it was the two of you quarrelled over all those years ago, and I don't want to know, but she's very upset about Jeremy—they've been friends since they were children. In fact, she probably cared a great deal more about him than you ever did."

Maddy blinked in shock at the unexpected line of attack. "Did...Sassy say I'd upset her?" she demanded, struggling to control her anger.

"No—she wouldn't say a word against you. But I could see for myself there was something going on. Just cut it out, OK? You might at least make an effort to be nice to her—she isn't strong, like you. She's very easily hurt."

Maddy could feel the anger simmering inside her, but she forced a saccharine smile. "Whatever you say," she conceded, not troubling to keep the edge of sarcasm from her voice. "How touching that you're so concerned about your ex-fiancée—even though only last week you were asking me to marry you."

"And you turned me down," he countered, a hint of danger in the sardonic smile that indented the corners of his mouth. "But even if you hadn't, there would be no reason for you to be jealous of Saskia—I told you, she and I are no more than friends."

"Jealous? Don't flatter yourself," she bit back at him caustically. "Your feelings for her are of even less interest to me than your feelings for me."

"Oh, really?" He laughed softly, his eyes glinting. "If it weren't such an inappropriate occasion, I might consider exploring that issue a little more...fully. However, the solicitor will be here in a few moments to formally read the will—it seemed the most convenient way to handle it, while everyone is here. I trust that meets with your approval?"

"Since you've presented me with a *fait accompli* I can hardly disagree, can I?" she pointed out with a touch of asperity. "I hope this isn't going to be typical of your idea of consultation?"

"I can assure you it won't be," he returned gravely.

Which very effectively took the wind out of her sails, when she had been itching to have a really good quarrel with him, she reflected, biting down on her irritation. "Thank you," she grated, and, turning her back on him, moved over to stare blankly out of the window.

"It might be best to have the reading in here," he suggested. "What do you think?"

"Good heavens, are you actually asking my opinion?" she queried cuttingly. She turned from the window to glance briefly around the room and shrugged. "Yes, certainly—if there'll be enough room."

"Oh, I think so, if I rearrange the chairs," he responded, ignoring her poisoned barbs. "It won't involve everyone—just the immediate family and a few others."

"Fine." She became aware that her hands were tightly clenched, and made a conscious effort to relax them, schooling her expression into one of cool neutrality as she watched him move the furniture around to accommodate the party.

"How are your business plans coming along?" he enquired, in a tone that she could have taken to be one of friendly interest.

"Oh . . . fine," she responded tautly. "I've spoken to my accountant, and she thinks it sounds like a reasonable proposition."

A flicker of faintly sardonic amusement passed behind those agate eyes. "Very good," he accorded. "What about start-up finance? For advertising—that sort of thing?"

"I shall be discussing that with the bank manager on Wednesday. I don't anticipate any difficulties."

One dark eyebrow lifted in surprise—it was more than apparent that he hadn't really taken her ideas seriously. "Very efficient," he acknowledged. "So you'll be ready to take your first customers quite soon, then?"

"In a few weeks," she asserted, with a little more confidence than she felt.

"As quickly as that? Won't you need to have the place decorated first?"

She shook her head. "Only a couple of rooms in the east wing—the old morning-room and the one next to it; they should be quite big enough to accommodate the number of people I'll be expecting to begin with. I can have a lock put on the door through to this side of the building, so that people can't just wander through. And the old kitchen garden will do as a car park—it'll need to be gravelled over... I trust you won't object to that?"

"It could hardly be in a worse state than it is now," he conceded. "Naturally any money you spend on the house will be financed out of the estate."

"Oh, no," she insisted firmly. "I would prefer to keep things strictly separate. Anything that is for the benefit of the business will be paid for out of the business account. And naturally I will keep you fully informed of the dates of any functions that will be taking place—I wouldn't want to inconvenience you in any way."

He shrugged his wide shoulders in casual dismissal. "Oh, you won't inconvenience me—I don't usually stay here for more than the odd night or two when I'm in Manchester, and now that you'll be moving in here... I assume you *will* be moving in?"

"Yes. At Easter, I expect. I'd like Jamie to go to the local school in the village—I hear it's very good. I was planning to move him from where he is anyway—the teachers try very hard, but the classes are really much too big for children of that age."

"You aren't planning to let him start at prep yet, then?"

"No, I am not," she returned with considerable force, "I don't want him boarding."

"Why not?" he queried in mild surprise. "Jerry and I both started at that age."

"Exactly."

"And what is that supposed to mean?"

"Well, you can hardly claim that it did either of you any good," she pointed out with a touch of asperity.

"On the contrary," he countered, coolly aloof. "We had an excellent education."

"Yes," she retorted, resolutely standing her ground; if he was planning to try to interfere in Jamie's education he would find he had come up against an immovable object. "It taught Jerry to be a permanent adolescent, always running away from responsibility, and it turned you into a——"

"Yes?" he prompted, his voice silky smooth.

Maddy felt the hot colour run into her cheeks. "Never mind," she mumbled, her eyes sliding evasively away from his.

"No, please," he insisted with deceptive cordiality. "I'm interested in your opinion of me. It might help me understand a little better why you were so swift to turn down my proposal of marriage. I'm still nursing a bruised ego from that, you know."

"Oh, really?" she countered, unable to keep the acid from her tongue. "Forgive me, but I take leave to doubt that. You gave me the impression that it was of no more importance to you than . . . some business deal."

"But then my business deals are usually *very* important," he argued in that soft, dangerous voice. "They frequently involve millions of pounds."

"I'm . . . quite sure they do," she responded, stiffening as he took a step towards her. "But even you can't possibly believe that . . . that's in the same league as discussing marriage."

"On the contrary. As I made plain to you, I would regard our marriage as a business contract—to be honoured on both sides, naturally. Of course, I would prefer that you didn't regard it in the light of a hostile take-over—it was intended to be more of a . . . friendly merger. An arrangement that would suit both our needs."

He was moving closer, and Maddy retreated defensively, only to find herself trapped within a corner of the bookshelves that lined the room. He laughed softly, putting up his hands at each side of her shoulders to bar her escape.

"As I said, I would *prefer* a friendly merger—although I'm quite prepared to settle for a hostile take-over, if you insist. But before you...reject my overtures, perhaps you would care to...reconsider my terms.''

His voice had become a husky purr, and with every breath the musky male scent of his body was drugging her senses. Maddy found herself gazing up into those deep-set agate eyes, mesmerised by the sensual spell he was spinning around her. How could she think straight when he was so close? How could she resist the power of his will...?

His mouth brushed over hers lightly, tantalisingly, and with a low groan she admitted defeat, her lips parting softly as she surrendered to the expected kiss. But instead he drew back, his eyes flickering with mocking contempt.

''Yes, you really would, wouldn't you?'' he sneered. ''Even on the day of your husband's funeral. Though I don't know why I should be surprised,'' he added coldly, ''considering the way you behaved on the day of your wedding. You really don't have any scruples, do you?''

Maddy felt her cheeks flame scarlet, but her eyes flashed in icy anger as she pushed him away. ''*I* don't have any scruples?'' she retorted. ''*You* were trying to kiss *me*! And Jeremy was your cousin—he thought the world of you. So that makes you every bit as bad as you're accusing me of being, doesn't it?''

He caught her shoulders, his angry laughter mocking. ''Oh, you don't need to pile on the guilt,'' he grated. ''Don't you think I know that I shouldn't want you the way I do? I shouldn't have then, and I shouldn't now. But at least I had the honesty not to go through with a marriage that would have been an empty charade.''

She stared up at him in blank surprise. ''Are you saying you broke off your engagement to Saskia because of me?''

"Let's just say that you were the catalyst," he responded, a hard edge to his voice. "It was pretty obvious that if I was lusting after you I wasn't ready to finish sowing my wild oats and settle down."

"You...shouldn't have been lusting after me," she protested raggedly. "I was your cousin's wife..."

"I wanted you from the first moment I saw you walking down those stairs," he growled. "Every time I look at you I want you. I've waited a long time—even after you left Jeremy I knew I couldn't come after you, because he was still in love with you. But now we're both free agents—we can do whatever we want. And I want to strip you naked, taste the sweetness of your soft, warm flesh, feel the ripeness of your breasts in my hands..."

He bent his head into the hollow of her shoulder, his hard white teeth biting sensuously into her skin, his hand rising to cup the weight of one aching breast, the pad of his thumb brushing tantalisingly across the tender, hardening peak. A shock of sizzling pleasure shafted through her, but in the same instant she knew that she couldn't allow herself to surrender to it—not today of all days. Not ever.

From somewhere she found the strength to push him away. "Leave me alone," she insisted, struggling to escape from him. "Don't ever touch me again..."

The door opened, and as if from a million miles away she heard Julia's voice. "Mr Jenkins is here to read the will. Are we ready? Good heavens...!" Her eyes took in the flushed and breathless state of the two occupants of the room and she stepped swiftly inside, closing the door behind her. "What's been going on?" she demanded in shocked tones. "Have you two been arguing?"

It was Leo who recovered first, a wry smile curving that hard mouth. "Let's just say that Maddy and I were having a . . . rather heated discussion," he responded blandly. "I'm afraid we didn't quite see eye to eye."

Julia's face betrayed a fleeting expression of satisfaction; no doubt she was hoping that they wouldn't be able to co-operate on anything about the house, and would end up agreeing to sell it to her by default, Maddy surmised shrewdly. Well, she would be disappointed; *nothing* would make her part with Hadley Park.

Holding her head up with dignity, she moved over to sit down—deliberately selecting the armchair by the fire as being the most prominent chair in the room. She had to let the Ratcliffes know that she was here, and that she meant business—she wouldn't let Leo intimidate her, or allow Julia to treat her as if she was of no account.

"Yes, I think we're ready, Julia," she announced, more than a match for her in frigid politeness. "Would you please ask everyone to come in?"

The older woman hesitated, glancing uncertainly from her to Leo, but he merely shrugged his wide shoulders, that hard mouth curved into one of those sardonic smiles. "Yes, Julia, ask everyone to come in," he conceded drily. With an air of casual unconcern that Maddy could only envy he walked across the room to the chiffonier and poured himself a drink.

Slanting them both a suspicious frown, Julia opened the door, her manner instantly transformed as she cheerfully ushered everyone into the room.

They all filed in: members of the family who could claim to have some interest in the proceedings, a few particularly close friends of Jeremy's, and behind them some of the estate servants—the pensioners and tenant farmers who had been expressly invited by the solicitor.

The latter group stood hesitantly around the outside of the circle of chairs; it looked like a scene from the Victorian era, Maddy reflected with a touch of acid humour—and she certainly wasn't going to let it go.

"Why, Mrs Douglas," she exclaimed, welcoming a very elderly lady who had been the housekeeper before Mrs Harris. "Do have a chair—I'm sure one of the younger men will be more than willing to give up theirs." She fixed one of Jeremy's other cousins with a pointed stare, and, blushing slightly, he rose to his feet to allow the frail pensioner to sit down.

A couple of the others took the hint, and there were a few moments of shuffling before the seating had been satisfactorily rearranged. Jamie was hovering uncertainly by the door, not certain if he was supposed to join the grown-ups or not, and Maddy beckoned him over to perch on her lap—it was *his* inheritance that was about to be ordained, and he had the right to be there, even if he couldn't understand it all yet.

The solicitor opened his briefcase and took out a thick wedge of papers, which he set down on the table beside him, and then checked his watch. "I don't anticipate that this will take more than half an hour," he began in ponderous tones. "I believe the main dispositions are already known to most of you, and I doubt that there's anything contentious about them. So I shall begin..."

It was all pretty dull, and after a while Jamie began to fidget, so Maddy let him get down from her lap and sit on the floor. The bequests were more or less as she had expected, and she found her mind wandering back over the years she had known Jeremy, remembering the good times. A wistful little smile curved her soft mouth; dear Jeremy—he had once admitted to her that though he had constantly claimed he wanted her back, in reality he preferred being able to do as he liked without the encumbrance of family ties.

So how come Leo had such an abysmally low opinion of her? He wouldn't have got it from Jeremy, and the facts hardly accounted for it—even given a prejudiced reading of them. From beneath her lashes she cast a meditative glance across the room towards him. He had taken a seat when the others had come in—and Saskia had promptly claimed the seat beside him; she was whispering softly to him as the solicitor droned on through the pages of the will, holding his attention as she had the other night at dinner.

That was the source of the poison, Maddy recognised with sudden sharp clarity—one drop at a time, sweetened with honey, the dose precisely measured to do its work undetected. She had had a long time to do it—five years, if not longer. And he would have been very receptive, already feeling guilty about hurting her by breaking off their engagement.

It was hard to believe that the girl she had once believed to be her best friend could be so two-faced behind her back—but then it had been hard to believe that she would have had an affair with her husband. Had it been her revenge, because she'd known that it was because of her—Maddy—that Leo had broken off their engagement?

But Saskia hadn't known that—she would certainly have said something if she had. No, it had been pure selfishness. Spoilt, particularly by her doting father, she genuinely believed that she was entitled to anything she wanted—and any fault in herself she projected on to others. So, to convince herself that she had done no wrong in having an affair with Jeremy, she had built up a case that Maddy was the wicked one, marrying him

solely for his money. It was immaterial that Leo knew
nothing about the affair—he had been a sympathetic ear,
someone on whom she could rehearse her self-
justification. And with the added bonus, of course, that
if he ever *should* find out what had happened, he would
be ready-primed with her side of the story!

Well, there was nothing Maddy could do about it
now—even if she wanted to. And she didn't want to—
she didn't care what he thought of her. The only reason
she would have anything to do with him was because he
was her co-trustee; and that was a misnomer if ever there
was one, she reflected with a bitter little smile—trust
didn't come into their relationship at all.

CHAPTER SIX

THERE was no mistaking the sound of that car engine; it purred down the drive like a great lazy lion, expending not a fraction of its power. Maddy, hard at work on the table decorations for a wedding reception that afternoon, glanced up in time to see the sleek silver shape of Leo's Aston Martin glide past the window of the old morning-room in the east wing, towards the wide carriage-sweep at the front of the house.

She hadn't known that he was coming back today— he hadn't bothered to let her know. But then he hadn't bothered to tell her he was going away either; she hadn't seen him after the funeral, and it had been almost a week before Julia had mentioned in passing that he was in Australia on business.

The past six weeks had been the busiest of her life. Between getting the unused rooms in the east wing into a useable state—she had even done some of the decorating herself, and made the curtains—she had had to spend time with the bank manager and arrange insurance cover, as well as negotiate with the licensee of the village pub to cover her for serving alcohol on the premises until she had time to apply to the magistrates for a licence of her own. And, on top of that, she had had an advertising leaflet printed, and bought new tablecloths—while continuing to meet the commitments she had already made for organising parties and arranging to sell the house in Manchester and move herself and Jamie lock, stock and barrel to Hadley Park.

What was Leo going to think of her progress? He had seemed to accept her ideas when she had first told him about them, but she had suspected even then that he hadn't taken her seriously—he had made it quite plain that he thought she was just dabbling, that what she was really after was another meal-ticket. Well, she was about to prove him wrong—and he wasn't the kind of man who liked to be proved wrong.

It hadn't been easy to stop herself thinking about him over these past six weeks. Some of the things he had said... Had he really wanted her from the beginning? A small shiver of heat ran through her every time she let herself dwell on the memory of the rare times they had met; though he still had his own rooms, on the second floor of the west wing, he had been abroad almost all the time she had been married to Jeremy, except for a few brief visits home.

The first time he had appeared she had been heavily pregnant—she hadn't been expecting him then, either— and when he had walked into the orangery where she was repotting a bougainvillaea she had been so startled that she had dropped the plant, shattering the pot and spilling compost all over the cool tiled floor. Stooping awkwardly to pick up the pieces under his cold gaze, she had been all fingers and thumbs, until he had told her in a peremptory tone to leave it and let him do it. She could still remember standing there, looking down at those wide shoulders and dark head as he had swept up the mess, feeling such an urgent desire to touch him that she had blushed scarlet in shame.

Then there had been Jamie's christening, when he had become his godfather, and a couple of Christmases. He hadn't ever spoken to her much, but sometimes she had glanced up and caught him watching her with those dark, disturbing eyes, and she had felt her heartbeat skip and start to race.

But he had never given her any reason to suppose that he was in the grip of some desperate desire for her; in fact, the idea of the cool, arrogant Leo Ratcliffe being gripped by any emotion that wasn't fully under his control was laughable. No, there had to be some other reason for that unlooked-for proposal—something that she suspected she wouldn't like.

With a wry shake of her head, she turned her attention back to the dainty vases of spring anemones she was arranging as centre-pieces for each table. There was no point in worrying about what was going on in Leo Ratcliffe's devious mind; she could only go ahead with her plans and hope that he wouldn't interfere. Anyway, with luck he would have some other fish to fry by now, and the whole crazy suggestion would have been forgotten...

"Quite a transformation."

Maddy glanced up as Leo appeared in the doorway, her features schooled into a façade of composure. "Thank you," she responded evenly.

He strolled into the room, casually surveying the freshly papered walls and the attractive table layout over which she had expended so much effort—pristine white table-cloths and fan-folded napkins, and every piece of glass and cutlery polished to a gleaming shine. "Very nice," he accorded. "You seem to have quite a talent for this sort of thing."

"I told you, I've arranged a lot of wedding-receptions," she reminded him, her tone light, though she was watching him warily from beneath her lashes. "I enjoy it."

His jaded eye took in the pretty three-tiered wedding-cake on the centre table, topped with a tiny marzipan chapel complete with bridal couple. "How romantic," he remarked, a heavy inflection of cynicism in his voice.

"Yes, it is," she countered coolly. "The couple who are getting married are in their seventies—they were childhood sweethearts until the war, when they were parted. Both of them thought the other one was dead, and they both got married to other people. They've lived just a few streets away from each other all these years without knowing it, until they met up again two years ago—completely by chance—in the outpatients department at the local hospital, of all things! Both of them had been widowed, and so they got together and fell in love all over again."

"How very touching!" he mocked lazily.

"I think it is," she retorted, stung. "Though of course I wouldn't expect you to understand—you don't know anything about love."

"While you're an expert?"

"I never said that." Damn him—he had been back barely five minutes, and already they were arguing again!

Those agate eyes glinted in provocative amusement at having succeeded in needling her. He strolled down the room, examining in closer detail the Royal Doulton china, the silver cutlery, the lead-crystal glasses that she had found in one of the store-rooms in the basement—if Jeremy had known they were there, he would no doubt have sold them. "You seem to be doing pretty well," he commented with some reluctant appreciation.

"I am," she confirmed with a hint of pride. "I had a wedding last week, and a company presentation dinner, and I've got several more lined up—as well as a couple of birthdays and engagements. And I'm planning a

Ghost Night—I've already sold nearly thirty tickets. And it's nearly all been by word of mouth—apart from a notice I put in the local paper, I haven't had to do any advertising at all.''

''Well done,'' he conceded, a faint smile curving the corners of that hard mouth. ''Are you making much profit?''

''I will,'' she countered tautly. Not enough yet to deal with the damp in the cellar, or to have the chimneys repaired and repointed, but it was a respectable beginning none the less.

He lifted one dark eyebrow in mild surprise at the forcefulness of her words. ''You seem very determined.''

''Yes, I am,'' she retorted. ''I told you—this house belongs to Jamie, and I intend to keep it that way.''

''Very creditable,'' he accorded, an inflection of lazy mockery in his voice. ''I'm beginning to think I may have underestimated you.''

She regarded him with wary suspicion. There was to be no truce, it seemed; he was still her enemy—and a very dangerous one.

He had moved down to the far end of the room, where the French windows looked out over the old walled kitchen-garden, now converted into a gravelled parking area for guests' cars. ''Unfortunately the news from the Inland Revenue isn't too good,'' he remarked in a casual tone, his hands in his pockets as he surveyed the changes she had made outside.

''Oh...?'' Maddy stiffened instinctively, ready for trouble.

''It appears that Julia was right—Jeremy hadn't paid a quarter of the death duties owing from when his own father died. I've just had the figures through.''

Maddy drew in a long, steadying breath. "How much is still owing?" she enquired. He told her, and she felt an unpleasant chill shiver through her—she had thought she was doing well, but really she was just whistling in the wind.

"There's a possibility we could appeal," Leo mused doubtfully. "The figures are based on a time when property prices were a good deal higher. But I don't hold out much hope."

Struggling to maintain an outward semblance of calm, she began clearing up the debris of stem-cuttings and stripped leaves from her flower-arranging, tidying them on to a sheet of old newspaper. "They...can't expect us to pay that all at once, can they?" she queried. "Surely we can pay by instalments?"

"Of course. And as Jamie's so young, it's likely that they'll allow quite a reasonable length of time. But it's still going to be very difficult for you."

"Yes..." She pulled a wry face. "At least the drop in property values will mean it won't be quite so much this time around—I was cursing it, because it's making it so difficult to get a decent price for our old house."

"Of course, there *is* still another alternative," he drawled, the cool indifference of his tone at odds with the sharp glint in his eyes.

"Oh...?"

"You could agree to marry me. That would solve all your financial problems at a stroke."

A small piece of oasis had fallen to the floor, and it was absolutely essential that she retrieve it immediately. By the time she sat up again, she felt reasonably confident that her voice would be under control. "I'm not sure that that's the kind of solution I'm looking for," she responded with cool dignity. "We agreed that I should take six months to see if I can make my business plans work out before we discussed it again.''

He lifted one dark eyebrow in sceptical enquiry. ''You still believe you can make enough money at this to keep the estate going?''

''I'm...not sure,'' she conceded cautiously. ''This latest piece of news about the death duties hasn't exactly helped, but if there are no more disasters like that I think I should be able to manage.''

''Very well—you have until August, then,'' he responded, the velvet cordiality of his tone in no way disguising the hardness that lay beneath it. ''In the meantime, I shall make arrangements to move my stuff out of my rooms.''

''You...don't have to do that on my account,'' she protested, determined not to let him see that his presence disturbed her in any way. ''You're quite welcome to go on using this place as a *pied-à-terre* for as long as you need it.''

''Ah, but I shall be wanting rather more than a *pied-à-terre*,'' he returned, an enigmatic glint in those deep-set eyes. ''I've decided to move my main base of operations to Manchester—that means I'll be spending a great deal more time here in the future. I'll take an apartment in town on a short-term lease until I come to some more...permanent arrangement.''

It took something of an effort of will to keep her smile fixed in place at this unwelcome news, but, having extended the initial invitation, to withdraw it would betray her fear. Besides, people would say that she had turned him out, when he had arguably as much right to be here as she did. ''But there's still no need for you to move out.'' It was proving difficult to keep her voice steady.

"Why don't you stay until you *have* established something more permanent?"

The hint of satisfaction in his smile confirmed her suspicion that he had intended to manoeuvre her into exactly this position. "That's very kind of you," he murmured. "If you're sure that it won't be an inconvenience?"

"Of course it won't," she asserted, with a shot of defiance against fate. "And I'm sure it would be what Jeremy would have wanted."

"And of course that would be a key point with you," he remarked silkily, "to take account of Jeremy's wishes."

She flashed him a fulminating glare. "I have no intention of discussing——"

Abruptly the door flew open, and Jamie bounced into the room. "Hi, Uncle Leo—you're back!"

"So it would appear," came the dry response.

Jamie grinned, quite unabashed by this welcome. "I saw your car, but you didn't see me. I was climbing the apple tree over by the corner outside the library."

"Jamie, I've told you not to climb that tree," Maddy reminded him sharply. "You might fall."

"Oh, it's not very high," Leo argued dismissively. "Jerry and I climbed it often enough when we were his age, and neither of us got more than a few bruises and scratches. So what have you been up to while I've been away, Half-pint?" he added, before Maddy's fury at his interference had subsided sufficiently for her to speak. "Had your nose glued to your computer, I suppose, while that confounded kitten of yours has been scratching all the furniture?"

"Sooty doesn't scratch things," the child assured him earnestly. "I've been teaching him to hunt for mice. And

I've been to see my new school—I'm starting after Easter. And they play rugby!''

"Rugger," Leo corrected him mildly. "And they won't play in the summer term."

"No, but then there'll be cricket. Uncle Leo," he added, his voice taking on a note that Maddy knew meant a wheedle was coming, "when I start, will you take me in your car—just the first day? *Please*?''

"No, Jamie," she interrupted firmly. "Uncle Leo is far too busy to drive you to school."

"Not at all," the infuriating man responded with a bland smile. "I'm sure I can fit it in."

"Oh, *thank* you!" Jamie cried excitedly. "The other kids'll be just *green* when they see it!"

Leo laughed, and ruffled his soft brown hair. "That's fixed, then," he promised. "Run along now, Half-pint—I suspect your mother is itching to haul me over the coals."

Jamie looked a little puzzled, but obeyed the casual command with a readiness that Maddy could only appreciate. But as the door closed the glare she turned on Leo would have frozen a volcano. "I told you before, I won't have you undermining my authority with my son," she ground out, her jaw taut with anger.

He returned her a placatory smile. "I'm not undermining your authority. You can't stop the kid climbing trees—unless you're planning to turn him into a milksop."

"I wasn't only referring to the tree. I said he wasn't to ask you to take him to school in your car."

"Oh, don't get your panties in a pinch about it," he taunted lazily. "It can be tough for a kid, starting a new school—they're like puppies in a litter at that age, all pushing and shoving for position. If turning up in my car can give him a bit of status to start him off with, where's the harm in it?"

"What a typical male attitude," she threw at him. "Teaching him to think about status symbols and competing with his peers at his age!"

"Unfortunately, that's a lot of what life's about," he responded evenly.

"Maybe. If that's the case, he'll learn about it soon enough. I'd like him to remain a child for at least a little while." And, sweeping up the bundle of flower debris, she stalked with magnificent dignity from the room.

Of course, it could have been no more than a coincidence that from the moment of Leo's return things began to go wrong, but as problem mounted on problem Maddy began to doubt it. First the local licensing committee turned down her application for a licence of her own to sell alcohol, so that she would no longer have to rely on the good nature of the publican in the village; the reason they gave was that she lacked sufficient experience, but even her solicitor was puzzled by that.

Then two party bookings were mysteriously cancelled. She was reluctant to challenge Leo openly by asking if he was behind this sudden down-turn in her fortunes, but she did try enquiring of him obliquely whether he knew either of the groups involved, and he flatly denied it. But she wasn't convinced; he wanted to marry her, for whatever reason, and although he had appeared quite unruffled by her refusals she couldn't help but fear that he would find a way to force her into compliance.

The one thing that puzzled her was *why* he wanted to marry her. Oh, she was quite sure he was cold-blooded enough to prefer the sort of clinical arrangement he had outlined to her; but surely there were other women of his acquaintance who could be persuaded to accept those terms? The answer to the riddle came from an unexpected quarter.

It was the day after Easter Monday. Jamie had prevailed upon Leo to take him to Alton Towers for an Easter treat, and while she would have enjoyed the spectacle of Leo on some of the more blood-curdling rides she chose to forgo the pleasure—and a full day in his company—in favour of a shopping trip to Manchester.

It was a while since she had had a chance to get into town, and although it was mostly window-shopping she did buy herself a silk shirt and some rather pretty underwear, as well as a new peach-coloured lipstick. She also got some T-shirts and half a dozen pairs of socks for Jamie—heaven only knew what he did to them, but even the toughest blend seemed to go into holes within a few weeks. After several hours, and with a fistful of shopping-bags, she was glad to find a table at her favourite coffee-bar and sit down.

She had just taken the first bite of a wickedly indulgent slice of pecan Danish when a familiar girlish voice made her drop a dollop of cream into her lap. "Maddy! Hello—fancy bumping into you! Do you...mind if I join you?" The query was diffidently framed, as if the speaker was afraid of having her head bitten off.

Maddy forced a taut smile, wishing she'd chosen a table a little further back from the window, where she wouldn't have been spotted. "Hello, Saskia," she responded, carefully scooping up the spilled cream with her napkin. "No, certainly—sit down."

The invitation was accepted with alacrity, and Saskia waved a waitress over. "I'll have a coffee, too, and...dare

I? That pastry looks delicious, but I have to watch my weight, you know. Oh, go on, I'll be a devil for once, shall I? Yes, I'll have one." She sighed as the waitress wrote down the order and left the table. "It's probably a big mistake—every bit I eat seems to go straight to my hips. You're so lucky—you're *so* slim. Don't you ever have to worry about putting on weight?"

"Not a great deal," Maddy responded mildly—dieting had been almost a competitive sport among most of the other girls at their school, but it had always seemed a particularly tedious preoccupation to her.

"So, tell me all your news," Saskia invited, her friendly tone somewhat at odds with the wary expression in her blue eyes. "Julia told me you've opened up the east wing. I used to love those great big rooms. We used to play there when we were children, Jeremy and me—he used to tell me it was haunted and terrified the living daylights out of me, the rotten thing. Once he dressed up in a white sheet and made all these horrible noises."

Maddy laughed drily, choosing to ignore the other girl's reference to her late husband entirely. "As a matter of fact, I'm rather hoping it *is* haunted," she remarked. "I've got a party of ghost-hunters coming next Friday for a sit-down dinner."

Saskia's eyes widened. "Really? That sounds exciting."

"Actually, it's going to be a lot of hard work," Maddy acknowledged with a touch of wry humour. "But still, it's excellent business."

"Oh, yes—Nigel mentioned something about you turning the house into some kind of restaurant," Saskia recalled with a slightly puzzled frown. "It seems a bit of an odd thing to do."

"I haven't turned it into a restaurant—I'm simply using a couple of rooms in the east wing as a venue for parties and business functions. I had to do something—I have to raise enough money to pay off two lots of death duties, as well as keep the place going."

Saskia nodded solemnly. "Oh, yes—Jeremy was always complaining about death duties. It doesn't seem fair, really—I mean, it's bad enough having your father die, without having to pay out thousands and thousands of pounds to the Government as well. Still, you'll be able to sell off that bit of land down by the main road, won't you? Jeremy said that'll be worth a fortune once they start building the factories."

"Factories?" Maddy repeated blankly. "What factories?"

"You know—they're supposed to be building an industrial estate down by the old mineworks. Jeremy said that once they've got the go-ahead the value of the land will rocket—it's worth loads more if you can build on it than it is just for farming and that."

"Is that so?" Maddy mused. And did Leo know about it? Of course he damned well did—he had just forgotten to mention it to her, no doubt! Well, it certainly explained a few things, anyway.

She knew the piece of land Saskia was talking about—forty or fifty acres of rough land, a lot of it covered by old slag-heaps, bordered by the road on one side and the railway on the other, barely good enough for grazing sheep. As agricultural land it was almost worthless, but if it were to be redesignated for industrial building... She tried to calculate the figures, but they made her head swim.

"And... when did Jeremy say all this was going to happen?" she enquired carefully.

"Oh, I'm not sure," Saskia responded with a vague wave of her hand. "You know what it's like with these things—they talk about them for ages and ages before they get round to doing anything. But I think he was hoping it was going to be quite soon—this year, anyway. He was planning to order a new car when he got back from his skiing trip—he wanted one like Leo's."

"He would," Maddy sighed in wry amusement—how typical of Jeremy to think first of spending the windfall on a car, instead of something more sensible.

"Talking of Leo..." Saskia went on brightly.

"Were we?"

"When will he be back?" the other girl continued, as if she hadn't heard that dry comment.

"Back?" Maddy frowned. "From where?"

"From Australia, of course."

Maddy hesitated; but after all, she had no reason to spare Saskia's feelings. "He's been back for over a week," she informed her bluntly.

"Oh..." Saskia's cheeks went pale, and then red. "I... wonder why he hasn't rung me, then?"

"Perhaps he's been busy?" Maddy suggested—it was hard not to feel sorry for Saskia when she looked so hurt.

"Perhaps... Or perhaps he's doing it deliberately." She brightened considerably at the thought. "You know what they're like, men—they say they'll phone you and then they don't, just in case it would make them look too keen. But you always know when they do that that they really *are* keen—otherwise they wouldn't do it."

Maddy was about to dispute this somewhat convoluted logic, but changed her mind; Saskia's theories on the male of the species had always been far too complicated for her to follow. Anyway, the waitress had arrived with Saskia's coffee and cake, and she promptly tucked into it with a relish that belied her earlier concern for her waistline.

"Mmm—this is scrummy!" she declared. "I think I'll have another one."

Leo and Jamie arrived home barely in time for tea. "Sorry we're late," Leo said as they came in. "The traffic was horrific all the way home."

"Oh, Mum, you should have come!" Jamie declared rapturously. "You'd have loved it! We went on *loads* of rides—they go really fast, and upside-down, and through the water and everything! What's for tea?"

"If you can eat anything else after the number of hamburgers and ice-creams you've had today...!" Leo chided him good naturedly.

"Yes, but that was *hours* ago," Jamie argued. "I'd better go and feed Sooty first, though, hadn't I? I expect he'll be waiting, and wondering why I'm late."

He hurried away to feed his kitten—Maddy had insisted that he should do this himself, to teach him responsibility. She turned to Leo, forcing herself to smile—it was too early yet to let him know what she suspected. "You must be tired out, after a day with that demon," she remarked. "Would you like a drink or something?"

A flicker of mocking amusement lit his eyes as he let them slide down over her in an appreciative appraisal. "Or something?" he taunted provocatively.

She returned him a look of pointed warning. "Brandy or whisky?" she specified, determined not to let him needle her when he had been so good to Jamie.

He shrugged his wide shoulders. "Whisky, then, please." He grinned, folding his length into one of the armchairs, his long legs stretched out in front of him, crossed at the ankle.

"Thank you for taking Jamie out today," she said as she brought him his whisky—straight, the way he liked it.

He laughed wryly. "As a matter of fact I quite enjoyed it—apart from the crowds. The little demon dragged me on all the worst rides—he wasn't afraid of any of them. He's got plenty of spunk."

"Yes. Too much, sometimes," she mused, a tinge of anxiety in her voice. "Like his father."

Leo shook his head. "Oh, I don't think you need to worry about that," he assured her gently. "He's a sensible kid—he knows where his limits are. Anyway, I'll keep an eye on him."

Maddy slanted him a covert look from beneath her lashes before turning away to pour her own drink—a small Martini. It would be nice to believe that she could have someone to share her worries about her son as he grew up—it wasn't easy, treading the fine line between keeping him safe and mollycoddling him.

But it could never be Leo Ratcliffe, she warned herself firmly; this interest in Jamie had an ulterior motive, just like everything else he did. He wanted that land, at its current market value, so that he could be the one to cash in—and it seemed that he was even prepared to use her son to get to her. With that sort of money involved, it would be very dangerous to allow herself to lower her guard, even for an instant.

"I saw Saskia in Manchester today," she remarked breezily as she returned to the other armchair.

"Oh, really?" he sounded neither interested nor concerned. "How's she keeping?"·

"Oh, she seemed very well. She asked me if you were back from Australia yet—she seemed quite surprised when I told her you'd been back for over a week." What she wouldn't give to know what went on behind those unreadable eyes! "She seemed to have been expecting you to call her."

He shrugged his wide shoulders in a gesture of casual dismissal, picking up the evening paper. "Oh, I expect I'll be seeing her some time within the next few days. By the way, I've promised to take Jamie to the safari park tomorrow. Do you mind?"

She blinked at him in surprise. "No, I don't mind— if you don't. That is, if you don't mind risking driving around it in your car, with the camels spitting at it and the monkeys trying to wrench the windscreen wipers off!"

He chuckled with laughter. "Oh, I've drawn the line at that," he assured her. "I'll take the old Land Rover. He'll be better off in that, anyway—being higher up, he'll be able to see more. Do you want to come?"

"Not particularly—if you don't mind taking him by yourself," she responded evenly. It was a risk to let Jamie spend so much time with him—he was already far more attached to him than she would have liked—but she didn't want to deny her son the treat. And anyway, Leo would soon be off on another business trip, or at least too busy to keep up this level of attention.

Besides, tomorrow she intended to do a little detective work at the local council offices; she needed to find out a little more about the plans for this industrial estate— exactly where it was to be, how big, how much of Hadley Park land might be under consideration for redesignation and when it was due to go before the planning committee for a final decision.

CHAPTER SEVEN

THE sleek silver-grey Aston Martin drew into the school gates to an awed reception from a dozen or so small boys, who gazed at it in reverent wonder. Jamie, in the back seat, visibly swelled with pride, but Maddy felt a twinge of embarrassment—the car looked so spectacularly out of place beside the 2CVs and Fiestas of the teaching staff.

As Leo climbed out the audience fell back—his imposing height must have made him quite intimidating to them, and though they were clearly itching to get a closer look at the car none of them wanted to risk being accused of getting sticky fingermarks on it. Jamie, however, was one of their peers, and they gathered around him eagerly.

"Is that your dad's car?" Maddy heard, breathed in tones of envy.

Jamie nodded, slanting her a swift look of pleading not to correct the slight inaccuracy. Her lips thinned, but she said nothing; the rituals of male status were an incomprehensible mystery to her, but she wasn't going to risk showing him up in front of his new class-mates on his first day by insisting that Leo was only his uncle—once he had found his feet there would be time enough to correct the misunderstanding.

There was something about a headmistress's office that could still evoke feelings of trepidation, but Mrs Lubcek was nothing like the Miss Pilkington of Maddy's own schooldays. A small, neat woman of around fifty, she had a stern but kind manner, and a ready smile as she ushered Maddy and Leo into her office.

"Ah, Mr and Mrs Ratcliffe—do come in. I'm so glad to see *both* of you—it's so important that fathers should take as much interest in their child's education as mothers."

Maddy felt a hot wave of colour sweep up over her cheeks. "Er... I..."

"I'm not actually Jamie's father," Leo supplied. "His late father was my cousin."

"Oh... I see. I'm so sorry." She quickly recovered her brisk manner, moving over to sit down at a large desk which was covered with piles of brightly coloured children's reading books and well-used exercise books full of the children's work. There were several paintings and collages on the walls, which were clearly also the work of the children; Maddy liked that—it was one thing to pin up their work in the corridors and classrooms, but to have it in here, in her own domain, suggested that this was a woman who was genuinely fond of children.

"Well, now, I expect you'd like to know which class Jamie will be in." She included Jamie himself in her smile. "I've decided to put you in Miss Kenny's class to begin with, and see how you get on. We don't have formal streaming," she added to Maddy, "but we do think quite carefully about which class to put the children in. However, judging by the results of his reading and arithmetic tests, I'm quite sure he'll be able to keep up."

Maddy nodded; she had known that it wasn't merely maternal pride that had convinced her that her son was particularly bright for his age.

"Miss Kenny will be along in a minute to meet Jamie, and take him along to his classroom. In the meantime, perhaps I could just take down a few particulars?'' She took some keys and unlocked a filing cabinet beside her desk, and took out a form. ''Just the basic information I need—the name of his doctor and things like that. Now, I have your name and address and telephone number. Is there anyone else I can contact in the event of an emergency, in case you're not available?''

Maddy hesitated, glancing reluctantly at Leo; after all, he was the obvious person. ''Er...I think Mr Ratcliffe...''

''Of course.'' Mrs Lubcek beamed in delight, and wrote down his name. ''Could I just have your address...?''

''It's the same as Mrs Ratcliffe's,'' he responded blandly.

The smile wavered only slightly, but she made no comment, simply writing it on the form. Maddy shot Leo a swift glare, but he merely lifted his shoulders in a small shrug—after all, there was nothing else he could say. And it was her own fault for trying to pretend that it didn't matter to her if he continued to live at Hadley Park—no doubt Mrs Lubcek wasn't the only one who would draw her own erroneous conclusions.

Jamie's new teacher turned out to be a pleasant and capable-looking young woman with soft, curling auburn hair—Maddy felt that she could entrust her boisterous son to her with little anxiety. ''Come along, then, Jamie, shall we go and meet the other boys and girls in your class?'' she suggested cheerfully, after being introduced to Maddy and Leo, and exchanging a few words. ''Say goodbye to your mother and fa—'' She cut off her slip of the tongue with a wry grin of apology.

''Bye, Uncle Leo,'' Jamie piped up, eager to be off on his new adventure. ''Bye, Mum.''

"See you later, Half-pint," Leo responded casually. "Be good."

"Goodbye..." But he was already halfway out of the door as Maddy spoke; perhaps he was too big now, after all, to kiss his mother in front of his teacher.

"Well, I think that's it, then," Mrs Lubcek announced brightly. "If you have any queries later, don't hesitate to pop in and see me—in fact, we positively encourage parents to come into school. And I hope we'll see *you* again, Mr Ratcliffe," she added, shaking his hand in farewell. "Even though you aren't his father, young Jamie is clearly very attached to you."

Leo smiled, turning on a megawatt charm. "I'm very attached to him," he concurred.

"Good. Well, goodbye—see both of you soon."

There was a certain clip in Maddy's step as she walked beside Leo down the lino-tiled passage that made him glance at her, one dark eyebrow lifted in sardonic enquiry. "Something wrong?" he asked.

"Should there be?" she bit back. "She only thinks we're living together."

He laughed softly, holding open the door for her to step out into the April sunshine. "Well, we are, in a sense," he pointed out. "Besides, she probably thought nothing of it—it's very common these days."

"It may well be," she retorted in a furious undertone, not wishing to argue with him too loudly so close to the classrooms. "But we *aren't*."

"Well, there's one way to regularise the situation," he reminded her, an inflexion of mocking humour in his voice.

"I am *not* going to marry you," she snapped as she waited for him to unlock the car door.

He shrugged those wide shoulders, a taunting smile curving the corners of his hard mouth. "Pity. It would have saved Jamie the problem of having to explain that this isn't exactly his *dad's* car."

"And I'm not going to let you use my son to get at me," she asserted fiercely. "That is just about the lowest..."

The glint in those agate eyes was a clear warning: he would use any tactic necessary to get what he wanted. And she was running out of strategies for her defence.

The trap was closing in on her even faster than she had anticipated. They arrived home from the school to find that the postman had been; one of the letters was from the London auction-house where she had sent a couple of paintings she had hoped might be Landseers, to tell her that they were not, the other was from the insurance company to say that they would not renew the policy unless the whole house was rewired.

"Problems?" Leo enquired.

Reluctantly she held out the letters to him. "You might as well see these—they relate to the estate."

He took them from her, and glanced over them. "Not looking too rosy, is it?" he commented, a hint of provocative amusement in his voice.

She returned him an icy glare, but chose not to enter into a discussion. She didn't want him to know yet that Saskia had told her about the land—he would only step up his campaign.

The next blow fell a couple of days later, when Bill Potton, the licensee at the pub in the village, who had been covering her for the sale of alcohol at her functions, rang to tell her that he could no longer provide this service. "It's not down to me," he excused himself gruffly. "It's the brewery—they say you're taking away my custom."

"But that's ridiculous!" she protested, on the point of desperation.

"I'm sorry, Mrs Ratcliffe." He was clearly anxious to terminate the conversation as quickly as possible. "If I was the tenant here I'd have a free hand, but I'm only the manager and they pay my wages—there's nothing I can do."

"All right. Well, thank you for at least letting me know," she responded bitterly, putting down the phone. Leo was in the library, and with her temper up she marched in there. "I don't suppose you happen to know the managing director of the local brewery?" she demanded.

He glanced up at her, a faint smile flickering across that firm, fascinating mouth. "No, I'm sorry, I don't. Why?"

"Oh, never mind—I don't suppose you'd admit it if you did!" And she slammed the door, running up to her own room, where if she was going to cry at least she could do it in privacy.

Disappointment and frustration were boiling inside her; she had worked so hard, and now it had all been wiped out. Even if she could find another licensee in the area who would be willing to help her, they were likely to be in the same position as Bill—beholden to the brewery that employed them.

Oh, she could carry on with the children's parties, of course, but that alone wouldn't be enough to keep her going. All the adults would expect alcoholic drinks to be served—at the very least to have wine with their meals. She would have to contact all her bookings and let them know, and they would almost certainly cancel.

The only thing she had left to hold on to was the land sale. Her enquiries at the council offices had brought her the information that the scheme was due to go before the planning committee in June. If she could just hold out until then.

On Friday afternoon she had one of her few remaining bookings—a party arranged by the local Twins and Triplets Club. Fortunately the weather was glorious, and she had booked a bouncy castle, which as usual was extremely popular with the children. It was a bit confusing seeing duplicates everywhere you looked—some of the parents were twins as well—and she was rushed off her feet all afternoon, but it was enormous fun.

The last of the families had gone by six o'clock, leaving her with the wearisome task of clearing up the mountains of debris. Jamie and two friends he had brought home from school with him came out cheerfully to help, in return for a private session on the bouncy castle before the men arrived to take it away, so that within quite a short time the garden and the old morning-room were reasonably tidy again.

"That's it!" she announced with a satisfied sigh, looking around to see if there were any more jobs that needed urgent attention before she sat down. "I'm going to collapse now. I'll use up those left-over sandwiches for tea, Mrs Harris—there's no need to cook anything just for me."

"All right, dear. You put your feet up—you've had a busy day. I'll make you a nice pot of tea, and the boy's just been by with the newspaper."

"Ah, good. That's just what I need—a nice lazy read and a cup of tea. I think I'll have it in the orangery instead of the dining-room."

The orangery was built on to the west wing of the house. It was years since oranges had been grown in there, but it had a rather spectacular bougainvillaea growing up the wall, and a good collection of exotic tropical tree-ferns. The sun had been on it for most of the afternoon, so it was lovely and warm, and the view over the gardens to the distant heights of the Peak District were really superb, especially in the soft glow of the setting sun.

Mrs Harris brought out a tray of tea and sandwiches, and Maddy sat at the white-painted cast-iron table, contentedly reading the paper. Things were difficult, but when she could sit out here like this, enjoying the serene panorama of green fields and waving trees and distant blue hills, she couldn't feel dissatisfied.

The news item was tucked away on an inside page: "Site Protesters Win Public Enquiry". She stared at it in shock, but with an uncomfortable sensation of inevitability; was this Leo, using his powerful influence again? A public enquiry could take more than a year. And she couldn't afford to wait that long for the money from the sale of the land—there were too many urgent debts pressing on her. But Leo could afford to wait.

She rose to her feet and moved over to the long glass-paned wall that looked out over the garden and the valley, her eyes misting with tears. She loved this house; from the first moment she had walked in here nine years ago, with Jeremy, it had felt like home. Even if it wasn't for Jamie, she would do almost anything to keep it.

Including marrying Leo? a small voice asked inside her head. Yes, even that—if his offer was still open. Unfortunately he was away this weekend, which meant she would have to wait until Monday. Well, at least that would give her time to be absolutely sure that she had no other options, she mused wryly. But, short of robbing a bank, she couldn't think of anything else that would solve her problems.

Something warm and furry rubbed itself around her ankles, and she looked down to see Jamie's little black kitten gazing earnestly up at her. She stooped and picked it up, laughing as it lapped at her hand with its rough little tongue. "You know, you should be a lucky cat," she remarked, holding it up to study it. "You're all black—there's not a single white hair on you. Will you bring me luck? I could do with some."

The kitten stared at her, puzzled, for a long moment, and then with what could have been a shrug leapt lightly down from her arms and walked away.

Maddy laughed wryly to herself. "Yes, that just about sums up my luck at the moment," she remarked. "It got up and walked away."

Leo arrived home late on Monday, just in time for dinner. It had been a nerve-racking weekend; Maddy had found it hard to sleep, hard to eat, hard to concentrate on anything. Her mind had played over endless scenarios of the encounter, and she had rehearsed and amended her script until she was sure she had the right words ready.

But when she walked out of the drawing-room into the hall to find him standing there, his briefcase still in his hand, flicking through the pile of post that was waiting for him on the sideboard, she caught her breath in shock. "Oh! I...I didn't hear your car," she stammered awkwardly.

"It had a slight problem with the ignition—I left it at the airport," he responded, that familiar sardonic humour glinting in his eyes as he let them drift down lazily over her body, taking in every slender curve.

"Good evening, Maddy—you're looking a little tired. Not been working too hard, I trust?"

Suddenly everything she had planned to say had gone out of her head. "No, I ... It's been ... No, I haven't," was all she could manage.

He slanted her a faintly quizzical look, but didn't pursue the issue. "I think I have time to change for dinner," he remarked, glancing at his watch. "I won't keep you waiting."

She watched him walk up the stairs, her mouth dry. Keep her waiting? She had waited for three days—surely she could survive another thirty minutes? But it was torture, her mind a prey to every kind of anxiety. With the sale of the land delayed indefinitely, and so many bills that she couldn't pay, he could simply force her to agree to sell the estate to him outright—he no longer needed to marry her. What if he just laughed at her, and said the offer was withdrawn? What if he demanded she go to bed with him right away?

By the time he came down again her nerves were stretched as taut as piano wires. He had discarded the jacket of his formal business suit and changed into a clean shirt, which, as he often did, he had left open at the collar and turned back at the cuffs, revealing a distracting glimpse of the smattering of dark, curling hair and bronzed skin at his throat and wrists.

Afraid that the wobbling of her legs would betray her agitation, she had already taken her place at the dining-table, and was absently pleating her napkin in her lap when he came in.

"I'm sorry—I hope I wasn't too long?" he enquired politely.

"Not ... at all," she managed with a forced smile. "Would you like some soup?"

"I'll get it. Some for you?"

"Er . . . Yes, please."

Mrs Harris had already left, returning to her own small cottage in the village, but she had put all the dishes on a heated trolley so that they could serve themselves. Leo lifted the cover from the tureen, and ladled out a generous serving for each of them.

"Mmm—chicken and sweetcorn," he remarked as the delicate aroma filled the air. "It's making my mouth water already."

Mrs Harris's cooking usually had that effect on Maddy, but tonight she had no appetite at all. She kept her eyes lowered as he placed the bowl in front of her, her hand shaking slightly as she picked up her spoon. "Did you . . . have a good trip?" she enquired, struggling to make conversation.

"Quite good, thank you. How was your weekend?"

"Oh . . . quiet. Jamie had some friends round—he seems to have settled into his new school very well."

"That's good."

She hesitated, desperately wishing that she could remember what she had been planning to say. It had been easy when he hadn't been there, to think of herself remaining cool and in control, but with him sitting opposite her she was far too physically aware of him—of that uncompromising maleness, underlined by the hard line of his jaw, the width of his shoulders.

"Is the soup a little too hot for you?"

"What? Oh . . . No, it's fine, thank you." She knew the strain was reflecting in her voice, but the more she tried to keep it steady the more edgy she sounded. "Is it . . . serious, whatever's wrong with your car?"

He shook his head, looking faintly amused by her uncharacteristic gaucheness. "No—a very minor problem.

Hopefully it will be fixed tomorrow, and I'll have it brought home. How's your car going?''

She pulled a wry face. "I think the clutch is slipping. I suppose I'll have to see about getting it repaired some time."

"Don't risk leaving it too long," he advised. "You don't want to get stranded."

"No. I'll...probably ring the garage tomorrow."

He was watching her across the table, that steady regard making her quiver inside. "Is there something wrong?" he queried.

"What...? Oh, no, nothing!" She forced a bright smile. "Nothing at all." Damn, at least that would have been some kind of opening. "Why?" she added a little belatedly.

His smile was lazy, knowing. "You just seem a little agitated, that's all. No more bills arrived?"

She shook her head. "No, thank goodness! I hope there won't be any more for a time now."

"Let's hope so."

After that the conversation lapsed into an uneasy silence. Maddy could hardly taste the delicious noisettes of lamb that Mrs Harris had so carefully prepared, or the tender vegetables, grown on the estate—she could have been eating ashes. The meal over, she was glad to accede to Leo's suggestion that they take their coffee into the drawing-room—perhaps in that slightly less formal setting she would find it easier to say what she had to say.

The drawing-room was large, but the way it was furnished made it feel quite cosy. There were three sofas, upholstered in a blue and yellow Chinese pattern chintz, grouped around the marble fireplace—and although it was the middle of April the weather was still quite cold, and a small fire had been lit, lending a soft glow to the room. The lamps were covered with yellow silk shades which gently diffused their light and the tall windows, which looked out over the garden, were hung with drapes of the same colour, now drawn.

Maddy moved across and sat down on one of the sofas, slipping off her shoes and tucking her feet up beneath her. Leo had sat down opposite her, putting his coffee on the low table beside him and moving a cushion behind his head. This was what it would be like, she mused, if she was married to him—sitting here in the evenings like this, perhaps watching television or listening to music, or reading a book...

Except that it wouldn't, she reminded herself bitterly—he wasn't looking for a marriage of domestic bliss. He wanted her for one thing only—he had made that perfectly clear. But she had no alternative—three uncomfortable days of trying to think of one had proved fruitless. If she was going to hold on to Hadley Park for Jamie, she had to go through with it.

It took a considerable effort to find enough control of her voice to speak, and when she did the words bore no resemblance to the careful script she had constructed in the safety of her room. "Your...proposal," she blurted out without any preamble. "Does it...still stand?"

He lifted one dark eyebrow in sardonic enquiry. "Do you mean do I still want to marry you?"

"Yes."

"Why?" he countered with a slow, mocking smile.

"Do you?" she persisted, her voice taut with agitation.

He took a moment to answer, his eyes sliding down over her in a cool, appraising survey, lingering with insolent intimacy on every slender curve. "Yes," he conceded at last. "I probably do."

She drew in a long, deep breath, struggling to steady the racing beat of her heart. "All right, then," she forced herself to say. "I'll...marry you."

"On the terms I outlined?"

She felt a hot blush of pink colour her cheeks. "Yes."

He accepted her acquiescence with a slight nod of his arrogant head, not troubling to question her about the reasons for her change of mind. Instead, rising easily to his feet, he crossed to the mahogany sideboard where the drinks were kept. "I think this calls for something more than coffee to toast our...future, don't you?" he enquired, a hint of provocative humour in his voice. "What would you like?"

"I'll have a brandy, please," she mumbled.

He brought it to her, but instead of giving her the glass he took her hand and drew her to her feet. "To us," he murmured tauntingly, clinking her glass with his, the glint in those agate eyes challenging her to drink.

She forced the brandy down her throat, though it almost choked her. Then he took the glass from her numb fingers and set it down on one of the tables, and putting his hands along each side of her face tilted it up towards him. She couldn't read the expression in his eyes, but she found herself caught in their spell, drowning...

His mouth came down on hers, warm and persuasive, his tongue sliding languorously along her lips, coaxing them part. She had to put up her hands against his chest to steady herself, feeling the hard resilience of muscle over bone and the soft, steady beat of his heart. The subtle musky scent of his skin was drugging her brain with every breath she took, and as his arms slid around her, curving her intimately close against him, she could only surrender.

His tongue was plundering deep into her mouth, expertly seeking out all the sweetest, most sensitive corners. And as she responded helplessly a sudden devastating realisation came to her. She was in love with him. That powerful tug of physical attraction she had felt from the first moment she had met him had been the warning, and over the years it had grown in secret—even during the time she hadn't seen him—and since they had met again, try as she might to deny it, it had virtually taken over her whole life.

But he didn't want her love—he only wanted her body. And she had just agreed to give it to him, whenever he wanted it, and to demand nothing in return. But not until they were married—she had that small respite at least. She drew back sharply, her breathing ragged but her eyes resolute.

"I've agreed to be... available to you, whenever you want me—once we're married," she forced out. "But I have to be sure that you'll keep to your side of the bargain before..."

He laughed—a harsh, mocking sound—and let her go. "Quite understandable," he conceded. "I shall make arrangements to settle the inheritance tax and any other outstanding bills immediately. And we'll announce our engagement at once. As for the wedding-date... There's really no reason to delay, is there? It only takes three weeks to obtain a licence—why don't we make it the Whitsun weekend?"

She sat down abruptly. "But... that's only a bit more than a month away!" she protested. "I... don't know if I can be ready as quickly as that. And... what about Jamie? I need time to explain it to him properly."

"Nonsense," he countered remorselessly. "Jamie will think it's a great idea. And as for being ready, there shouldn't be too much to do—unless you want a huge affair like your first one, of course?"

"Oh, no," she responded with a slight shudder. "Let's keep it small."

"I agree—just close family and friends. But in the village church, of course—I hope you didn't have a register office do in mind?"

She shook her head, feeling slightly faint. The end of May—it seemed so soon. But perhaps it would be best to get it over with. A small, hysterical laugh bubbled to her lips; it wasn't a case of getting it over with—the wedding would be just the beginning. The beginning of what, she didn't dare even let herself ponder.

She should have known that Jamie would greet the news of her marriage to his adored Uncle Leo with whoops of delight. In other quarters, however, the information created a furore. Julia was furious, accusing her in a hissing telephone conversation of being a scheming, gold-digging little whore—words Maddy was quite astonished to hear her use, though she wasn't at all surprised by the sentiment.

Saskia's reaction, too, was predictable. She came round to the house on the day after the announcement was made, catching Maddy in the garden rather belatedly pruning the roses. "Is it true?" she demanded fiercely, not even bothering to say hello.

Maddy smiled wryly, reaching over with the secateurs to take out a straggling twig from her favourite Elizabeth of Glamis rose. "Yes, it's true," she confirmed, her tone carefully neutral.

"You *bitch*," Saskia spat, so beside herself with rage that Maddy made ready to defend herself from those cat-like talons. "You stole Jeremy from me, and now you've stolen Leo!"

Maddy stared at her incredulously. "I stole *Jeremy* from you?" she repeated. "It may have escaped your memory, but you were engaged to Leo when I met Jeremy. And as for stealing Leo, I'm afraid you're deluding yourself if you ever thought he was yours to be stolen."

"I could have married him if you hadn't shown up again," Saskia asserted with bitter chagrin. "He's only marrying you for the money, you know."

Maddy laughed at that, shaking her head. "He's the one with the money," she reminded her. "I'm the one without it."

"But you own the house," Saskia insisted. "And don't tell me that it's really Jamie's, because it amounts to the same thing. The Ratcliffes have a thing about Hadley Park—they've owned it forever. I knew when he went on living here after you came back that you were up to something, but I never thought you'd do this to me. You knew I loved him..."

"Oh, no, I didn't," Maddy retorted, savagely blunt. "I knew you wanted him—or rather his money. But you never loved him—not before, and not now. You don't know how to love anyone but yourself."

Saskia's pretty face was contorted with rage and hatred. "You haven't won yet," she declared. "There's still a month to go—I could get him back in that time. I got Jeremy back—you couldn't hang on to him. He couldn't wait to come back to me when you were all fat and pregnant. I could get Leo back."

"Try," Maddy challenged her, her own voice laced with acid.

"I will!" Saskia flounced. "And I'll get him back—you'll see."

Maddy watched wryly as she stalked away. If she only knew the real reason why Leo was marrying her! She had only just worked it out herself. She had been a little puzzled about why he still wanted to go through with it, when he could get his hands on the house and its potentially valuable estate anyway—and his claims of an overpowering physical desire for her rang even less true, since he had so readily accepted her refusal to sleep with him before the wedding.

No, the truth was even more sinister. He believed that she had cold-bloodedly entrapped his cousin into marriage to provide herself with a meal-ticket, that she had made him unhappy, that maybe she had even contributed to his death. And so he was intent on punishing her on behalf of Jeremy; their marriage would be one not of love, as she had once dreamed, but of bitterness and revenge.

CHAPTER EIGHT

WHERE had the time gone? Maddy sat at her dressing-table, regarding her reflection in the mirror; she had had over a month, and now it was less than twenty-four hours. No miracle had occurred; no fairy godmother had waved a magic wand and deposited a very large cheque in her lap and Leo hadn't changed his attitude towards her one bit.

It was probably fortunate that he had been away for much of the intervening weeks, first to Europe and then to Hong Kong. He had arrived back from the latest trip only this morning, and after sleeping until lunchtime had spent the afternoon checking the installation of the very sophisticated computer and communications systems that had been installed while he was away—watched by a totally fascinated Jamie.

She had been hoping that he might have been going out tonight—his stag night—but apparently he had decided not to follow the tradition, and would be dining at home. Which meant that she had better get herself downstairs or she would be late—and that was bound to draw some sort of sarcastic comment from him.

Rising to her feet, she checked her reflection a last time; she had lost a little weight over the past few weeks—to some extent she could disguise it beneath the loose knitted jacket she wore over a simple blouse and skirt, but even the most skillfully applied make-up couldn't conceal the sculpted hollows beneath her cheekbones that made her grey eyes look huge in her pale face.

She was on her way downstairs when Jamie came careering in at full tilt from the morning-room, his small face white with distress. "Uncle Leo...!" He ran past her without a check, intent on one thing only.

"Jamie?" she called after him anxiously. "What's wrong?"

"It's Sooty—he's stuck up a tree and I can't get him down. Uncle Le—— Oh, there you are. Come quickly—he's stuck on a high branch, and he's crying."

Leo regarded him with tolerant amusement. "All right, Half-pint, there's no need to panic. He's probably perfectly all right—cats climb trees all the time."

"But he's just a kitten," Jamie persisted, struggling to hold back his tears, "And he's crying. Oh, please, Uncle Leo, come and rescue him."

With a wry smile, Leo conceded, allowing himself to be dragged by the hand through the morning-room and out of the French windows, to an old horse chestnut tree in the garden. A pathetic meowing was issuing from its branches; the little black kitten was about twenty feet from the ground, looking down with all the appearance of acute vertigo.

"He'll probably come down by himself if we leave him alone and don't panic him," Maddy suggested, with little hope of calming her son's anxiety.

"He's been up there for ages already," Jamie protested. "And it'll be dark soon—if we don't get him down he'll be up there all night. Can you get him, Uncle Leo?" He gazed up at his demi-god with pleading eyes that couldn't be ignored.

Leo slanted Maddy a fleeting glance of self-mocking humour—he really had no option but to live up to the child's expectations. "I'll go and fetch a stepladder."

It was no easy task. The stepladder was only fifteen feet long, which meant that there was an awkward climb through the branches to reach the kitten. Maddy stood at the bottom, holding it steady, watching with her lip between her teeth as Leo perched precariously, patiently trying to coax the scared little thing to wait while he reached up for it.

A frightened squeal, and a very rude word, told her that the mission had been accomplished—albeit with slight injuries to the rescuer, which when he finally got to the ground turned out to be a nasty scratch on his hand. He handed the kitten over to Jamie, who cuddled it solicitously as he hurried away to give it a comforting saucer of milk.

"Thank you," Maddy murmured; she hadn't wanted to be beholden to him, tonight of all nights—she had wanted to nurse her sense of grievance against him.

The glint of knowing amusement in those agate eyes indicated that he was fully aware of her feelings. "Think nothing of it," he responded drily.

"I'd...better put some antiseptic on that scratch," she offered.

"No need to bother," he assured her, sucking away the blood. "It's not very deep—I think I'll live." He glanced at his watch. "I'd better put this ladder away— dinner will be getting cold."

It would have been impossible, after that incident, to maintain the kind of aloof silence she would have preferred over dinner—and even more impossible with Jamie between them, chirping away like a cricket. He was particularly excited because he was going on a camping trip with his school over half-term, which had fortunately coincided with the date of the wedding, relieving them of the need to choose between leaving him with Julia or taking him with them on their honeymoon.

"What happens in a tent if it rains, Uncle Leo?" he wanted to know, his small face alight with lively curiosity.

"It stays dry—so long as you don't touch the canvas."

He frowned, earnestly puzzling this out. "Why mustn't you touch the canvas?"

"Because..." Leo's eyes searched the ceiling for inspiration on how to explain the scientific principles of surface tension to a seven-year-old. "You know what happens when you touch a bubble?"

"It breaks."

"Exactly. And the same thing happens with a drop of water if you touch it—it breaks. So if, when you're inside the tent, you touch the drops on the outside through the canvas they break, and then they can get through."

"And you get soaking wet!" Jamie gurgled, with a delight that Maddy suspected was a warning that he was longing for it to rain so that he could put the theory to the test. "Don't you wish you were coming camping too?"

"Er... No," Leo responded, straight-faced. "But no doubt you'll tell us all about it when you get back..."

The chirp of his mobile phone, resting on the sideboard, cut off any further discussion. He leaned over and picked it up. "Ratcliffe... Oh, hello, Sass..." His tone changed quickly from business-brisk to gentle concern. "Yes, all right, just calm down a moment and tell me what's wrong..."

Maddy could hear Saskia's voice, wailing and hysterical, on the other end of the phone, though she couldn't catch what was being said. But she could imagine; this was some kind of frantic last-ditch attempt to do as she'd threatened—to get the wedding called off, to win him back. Could he really not see through the scheming little bitch? Maddy wondered incredulously as she listened to him patiently trying to soothe the other girl's agitation. Apparently not... Or maybe he didn't want to.

"All right, Sass, I'll come over... Yes, I'm on my way right now. Just keep the door locked till I get there." He turned the phone off and rose to his feet, those hard agate eyes unreadable. "I have to go out for a while," he explained somewhat unnecessarily. "Goodnight, Half-pint—see you in the morning. I'm not sure what time I'll be back, Maddy."

She shrugged her slim shoulders in a gesture of the most supreme indifference, her jaw taut with angry frustration. "Don't worry—I shan't wait up for you," she assured him acidly.

Just like that—Saskia snapped her fingers, and he went running! Not that she actually *cared* of course—the only reason she was concerned that he might call off the wedding at the last minute was because she needed him to settle the outstanding debts, as he had agreed. And, of course, because Jamie was so fond of him, and would be dreadfully disappointed. Otherwise she would have been more than delighted for Saskia to have had him back.

It was late when the distinctive sound of the Aston Martin's powerful engine told Maddy that Leo was home— past midnight, according to the ornate Italian ormolu clock on the mantelpiece. She rose swiftly from her chair to turn off the television—she had been watching the late film, though she probably couldn't have related its plot or named any of the stars—intending to slip upstairs before he came in.

But with a wry smile she recognised that he would have seen the light on, and would probably catch her scuttling ignominiously across the hall. Sitting down again, she adopted a reclining pose, pretending to be absorbed by the comic antics of the hard-pressed American detective on the screen.

If she had hoped that he might go straight up to bed, she was disappointed. The door swung open and he leaned his wide shoulder against the jamb, regarding her with a sardonic smile. "Good evening. I thought you weren't going to wait up."

She flickered a brief glance towards him, and turned her attention back to the television. "I was watching the film," she responded coolly.

He strolled across to glance at the screen. "This one? Good heavens, haven't you seen it before? It's been on a dozen times."

"It's funny," she returned with a casual shrug. "I felt like being amused." The leading character had just crashed through a plate-glass window, and she forced a laugh, knowing that it sounded strained.

Leo moved across to the drinks cabinet and poured himself a generous slug from the whiskey decanter. "You realise, of course, that this is supposed to be terribly bad luck?" he queried, sitting down on one of the other sofas. "The groom seeing the bride on the wedding-day."

"If I'd realised you were coming home, I'd have gone up earlier," she informed him with studied indifference. "I assumed you'd be staying out all night."

"Oh? And why should you assume that?" he challenged, a glint of mocking amusement in those agate eyes.

"Well, poor Saskia sounded *so* distraught on the phone. What was the matter? Was there a spider in the bath?"

"As a matter of fact she'd heard some strange noises outside, and they'd frightened her," he responded, a hint of impatience in his voice. "She thought it was a prowler."

"Ah, poor thing," Maddy retorted on a note of biting sarcasm. "And did you find anyone?"

"No," he grated. "Possibly the sound of my car drawing up frightened them away."

"Quite understandable," she purred, the honey spooned on thick. "And then, of course, Sass invited you in for coffee, and begged you to stay until her nerves were feeling a little better?"

"Do you know, you almost sound as if you're jealous?" he taunted. "Now, why could that be, I wonder? After all, you're only marrying me for my money, aren't you?"

"Of course," she retorted sharply. "But I'd prefer it if it didn't get around that you'd spent your last night of freedom with your ex-fiancée. You know how people love to talk."

"And make a mountain out of a molehill?" he queried provocatively.

She slanted him a look of icy disdain. "I really don't care if it's a mountain or a molehill," she returned. "So far as I'm concerned, if you want to sleep with Saskia that's entirely your own affair—if you'll excuse the pun."

"I told you before, I don't want to sleep with Saskia—or at least not enough to put up with her constant demands. I had enough of that before—she's enough to drive a man half out of his skull, wanting attention the whole time and sulking if she doesn't get it. I want a woman who won't cling or make a fuss."

"Who'll just be available whenever you want her in your bed, and the rest of the time will quietly disappear into the woodwork?"

"Exactly." He lifted his glass, swirling the amber spirit around. "An entirely satisfactory arrangement."

Maddy felt a cold shiver run through her. "Do you always use people as ruthlessly as this?" she queried tautly.

"Ruthlessly?" One dark eyebrow lifted in mild surprise. "I haven't forced you into anything. You'll be doing extremely well out of the bargain."

"That depends on what you value most," she countered, her voice laced with bitterness. "Money, or self-respect."

A faint smile curved that hard mouth. "Stop acting like an outraged nun," he advised mockingly. "You made your choice. Do you want to change your mind? It isn't too late, you know. True, it would be a little...embarrassing to call the whole thing off at the last minute, but..."

She dragged in a deep, ragged breath, struggling to retain at least some semblance of composure. "You know I can't afford to keep the house unless I marry you," she responded stiffly. "And I'll keep to the agreement we made, so long as you keep to yours." She rose to her feet. "I'm...going to bed now," she managed. "I'll see you...tomorrow."

"Today," he reminded her, glancing at the clock. "It won't be very long now."

No, it wouldn't. The wedding was at two o'clock—just a little over thirteen hours away. And tomorrow night she would be in his bed. Once she had dreamed of it, guiltily wanting him, but now... "Goodnight," she ground out, knowing that the flush of her cheeks betrayed her thoughts. "I'll... leave you to turn off the television when you go up to bed."

"Sleep well," he murmured provocatively.

"I will," she retorted, and, tilting up her chin in haughty pride, she made her escape from the room, closing the door softly behind her.

The clock on the bedside table was ticking loudly, remorselessly ticking away the seconds, the minutes. Maddy had lain awake for more than an hour, staring at the shadowed ceiling, her mind a cauldron of emotions.

It was like waiting for the Sword of Damocles to fall. In less than twelve hours she would be standing at the altar to make her vows—and Leo Ratcliffe would certainly make sure that she delivered on her side of their bargain. With a low groan she rolled over in bed, hugging the pillow, the memory of the way he had kissed her, caressed her, so vivid that she could almost feel his hands on her body again.

It was the waiting that was the worst. If only she could get it over! Tomorrow she was going to have to put on a smiling face to the world, while inside her the terrible anticipation was building to a fever. And then, when the time finally came...

Abruptly she sat up. She was going to have to face it, and it might as well be sooner rather than later. At least, too, by choosing the time herself instead of waiting passively for him to come to her and demand her surrender, she could have some semblance of control over the situation—even if it was only an illusory control. Slipping out of bed, she shrugged off her nightgown and dropped it on to a chair, and then, picking up her peach silk wrap, she pulled it around her bare shoulders, tying the belt tightly around her waist.

She hadn't heard Leo come up to bed yet. Her mouth was dry as she stepped out into the darkened corridor, maybe she was crazy to be doing this, but she couldn't just lie in bed, unable to sleep, her mind a prey to all those disturbing images that were swirling into it. Better to get it over as quickly as possible...

The door of the drawing-room stood just slightly ajar; music was playing—the soft, smoky blues sound of New Orleans jazz—and the subtle glow of one of the silk-shaded lamps spilled out into the hall. Maddy hesitated, not sure—now that she was here—that she wanted to go through with this after all.

"Why don't you come in?" Leo's voice held a note of sardonic humour; he couldn't see her, but he must have heard her come downstairs.

She pushed the door open a little further. He was lounging in one of the big, comfortable sofas, his long legs stretched in front of him and crossed at the ankle, a thick-bottomed tumbler of whisky in his hand. Across the room, those deep-set agate eyes regarded her with faintly mocking amusement.

"Good evening," he greeted her cordially. "Having trouble sleeping?"

"A little," she conceded, the tension that was knotting inside her betrayed in her voice.

"Why don't you get yourself a drink?" he invited. "It might help."

She shrugged her slim shoulders and crossed the room to the drinks-cabinet, which stood open, the whisky decanter at the front instead of in its usual place. It was usually kept full, but now it was half-empty. "You must be having even worse trouble sleeping than me," she remarked, a hint of acid in her voice. "You've gone through nearly half a bottle. You'll have a dreadful hangover tomorrow."

He laughed without humour. "Don't worry—I won't leave you standing at the altar," he assured her. "Or were you hoping that I would?"

She slanted him a glittering glance from beneath her lashes. "You know I don't want to marry you," she responded tautly. "If I had any choice, it's the last thing I'd do."

"Is that so?" he taunted, watching her over the rim of his tumbler as he downed a thick slug of whisky. "Funny—there've been times I've received the distinct impression that you would quite enjoy it."

She had poured herself a careful single measure of whisky, but on second thoughts topped it up to what must have been at least a triple—tonight she needed a little artificial support for her courage. "Did you?" she ground out, moving to the sofa opposite him and tucking her feet up beneath her. "That doesn't surprise me. You're more than arrogant enough to interpret any kind of response on my part as enjoyment."

This time his laughter held genuine amusement. "Are you trying to tell me that you *haven't* enjoyed our...encounters?" he challenged provocatively. "Forgive me, but that's pushing my credulity a little too far."

She could feel the warmth of a blush creeping into her cheeks. "Oh, I won't deny that on a certain, purely physical level ... But it's about as meaningful as eating a strawberry sundae—a few minutes' pleasure, but no real satisfaction."

He lifted one dark eyebrow in quizzical amusement. "An interesting simile. But then you've barely tasted the ice-cream yet. Wait till you've tried the fruit—you might find its sweetness positively addictive."

She returned him a coolly level look. "I doubt it. This is going to be no more than a business transaction. That's the way you wanted it, isn't it?"

"More or less," he concurred, a faintly sardonic smile curving that hard mouth.

"Good." She tipped back her glass, the whisky hitting the back of her throat like fire as she drained it in one gulp. "Then there doesn't seem a lot of point in waiting until tomorrow, does there?" She rose to her feet a little unsteadily, and with hands that fumbled slightly dragged at the belt of her wrap. As she unfastened it, and let it slide back from her shoulders, she held his dark gaze defiantly. "This is what you wanted, isn't it?" she challenged him, naked as the wrap slipped to the floor around her feet. "Well? Is it worth what you're paying?"

The soft glow of the lamp was warm on her creamy skin, and she was conscious of the firm swell of her breasts as her tender pink nipples ripened beneath his level gaze, her stomach fluttering slightly in apprehension as his eyes drifted slowly downwards over its peach-smooth curve, to linger over the soft mound of blonde curls that crowned her slim thighs.

He took another sip of his whisky, his tongue savouring its mellow smoothness with much the same Epicurean appreciation as his eyes savoured her naked curves. Maddy swallowed hard, forcing herself to resist the temptation to snatch up her wrap and run from the room. She would have to face this—tomorrow night if not tonight. The music was soft and sensuous, a husky tenor

saxophone, and she let its languorous notes seep into
her, mingling with the hot alcohol in her bloodstream
to drug her mind.

He hadn't spoken; he was lounging back in the sofa,
totally relaxed, waiting silently to see what she would do
next. Slowly—very slowly, her body swaying with the
rhythms of the soft, sweet jazz—she moved towards him,
her eyes glittering beneath her lowered lashes. And then,
with a boldness she had doubted she could possess, she
stepped across his outstretched legs, confronting him
with the wanton invitation of an odalisque, offering every
facility of her body for her master's pleasure.

She was close enough for him merely to lift his hand
to touch her, but he didn't—he took another sip of his
whisky, only the glint of his eyes telling her that he was
amused by this reversal in the role of seducer. But now
that she had started this, some kind of ancient instinct
had taken her over, drowning out all trace of inhibition,
urging her on.

As she took the glass out of his hand and set it down
on the low table beside him he quirked one eyebrow in
quizzical enquiry, as if he still half believed that she
wouldn't dare finish what she had started. A small smile,
born of a certainty that she would, curved her soft
mouth, and she moved forward again to kneel straddled
across his lap, her fingertips resting lightly against his
chest.

His tie was hanging loose beneath the unfastened collar
of his shirt, and she tugged on one end of it so that it
snaked round and off; then she dropped it casually on
the floor.

"Careful," he warned, a hint of provocative humour
in his voice. "That's one of my favourite ties."

"I don't give a damn about your bloody tie," she retorted tigerishly, and turned her attention to the buttons of his shirt.

Ever since the very first time they had met, this was something she had always wanted to do—to unfasten his shirt and feast her eyes on the rough, dark, male hair that grew across his wide chest, on the smooth, hard muscles beneath his bronzed skin. She had had an impression, of course, to whet her appetite—she knew the general outline, knew the texture of his skin, and his habit of taking off his tie and leaving his collar open had frequently let her catch a tantalising glimpse of a few dark curls at the base of his throat. But now... she could smooth the fine cotton of his shirt aside, feel the thrill of touching him, of sliding her palms over the warm, hair-roughened contours...

With a low, hungry moan she leaned forward, bending her head to press her parted lips against the hard line of his collar-bone, breathing deeply of the subtle musky scent of his skin. She could feel his heartbeat beneath her fingertips, strong and steady, but when she slanted a swift glance up at him she saw that he had closed his eyes, and knew that he wasn't entirely indifferent to what she was doing.

The soft glow of the lamp cast shadows across his face, highlighting the sharp angle of his cheekbones, the slightly aquiline crook of his nose. His jaw was darkened with the faint rasp of his beard, but his lashes were as thick and silky as a girl's, and though his hair was brushed back from his forehead a single wayward lock had curled forward. And his mouth was firm and temptingly sensuous... and tasted of whisky.

He let her kiss him, let her probe her tongue into the corners of his lips, let her coax her way in to challenge his own to battle. And then abruptly he took control, one hand tangling in her hair to hold her captive, the other sliding down over the smooth curves of her naked body as she quivered in helpless response.

Now he was kissing her with a fierce demand, his tongue plundering deep into the sweet, defenceless valley of her mouth, taking all that she had offered and more. His hand had smoothed back up over her flank, rising with unmistakable intent to cup and mould the warm, ripe swell of her breast, the pad of his thumb rolling over the taut, tender bud of her nipple.

A sudden jolt of panic ripped through her, and she tried to draw back, but he refused to release her, his insistent grip on her hair reminding her that she had put herself in this position willingly. He caught her nipple between his thumb and finger, pinching it and twisting it, inflicting a torture of pleasure on the very borders of pain, making her gasp as the sizzling shock shafted like white fire into her brain.

He laughed in husky satisfaction, knowing that he inevitably had the upper hand, and lifted her so that her breasts were level with his face. Now he could use both his hands in that exquisite teasing, watching the response as her nipples darkened and her skin flushed. Her breathing was ragged, and her head tipped back as the smoky music swirled around her, evocatively sensual.

And then, as he lapped one ripe, succulent nipple with his languorous tongue, a sobbing sigh escaped her lips, and she arched her back to offer herself even more invitingly to the sweet pleasure of his mouth. She felt the light nip of his teeth, tugging playfully, first at one rosy peak and then the other, until at last he took one deep into his mouth to suckle at it with a hot, hungry rhythm that melted her spine to liquid honey.

She had left herself with no defences against him, her slender thighs spread wide as she straddled across his lap, exposing the soft, vulnerable cleft of velvet between to the most intimate caresses. And as his hand slid down over the smooth contours of her body she knew his intention, and a small shiver of apprehension rippled through her.

He let his fingertips trail slowly up over the silken flesh of her inner thigh, savouring its texture, tantalising her with a deliberate protraction of the moment of exquisite anticipation. She heard her own voice, pleading brokenly for his touch; if he had meant to force her to admit that she really did enjoy this purely physical level of pleasure he could not have succeeded better.

But it was more than just physical. She had been fooling herself, maybe from the very first time she had met him, guilt and pride denying the incontrovertible truth. She was giving herself to him because she loved him—and that was the greatest torture of all. Because she knew that all he wanted was her body. Her heart, her soul, her spirit didn't interest him in the slightest— he would discard them with the most careless contempt if she ever let him know that they were his. This was all she could have—and it was searing her soul to surrender to it.

His touch was tender, infinitely skilled, exploring the moist, tender folds to find the tiny hidden seed-pearl of pleasure that lay within them, stirring it into instant, electric arousal. She drew in a sharp breath, startled by the unfamiliar sensation, and then by the wave of response that engulfed her, pulsing through her veins as she fell dizzily against him.

She had known what it was like to want him, known the aching hunger of the long, empty years, but nothing could be like this craving—fierce and primeval—to feel the hard, urgent thrust of his possession. She moved against him in instinctive supplication, moaning as his thumb continued its sweet, arousing caress while his fingers dipped deep inside her, making her ready for the demands to come.

She whimpered in protest as he seemed to pause, but it was only to lay her down on her back on the thick Chinese silk rug in front of the fireplace. Her eyes flickered open, to see him looking down at her, his own eyes burning with the smouldering desire that she had so recklessly kindled into flame.

"This is how *you* wanted it," he reminded her ruthlessly, his hand moving to unbuckle his belt. "Right here on the floor—we're not going to make it as far as the bedroom. And just in case you're still wondering—yes, you are worth the money."

A bitter wave of humiliation swept through her. But she had known it would be like this, and she could only surrender as his weight crushed her beneath him and his strong thighs spread hers wide apart. She arched her back, offering herself to him willingly, and he laughed in harsh male triumph as he took her with one deep, powerful thrust that almost took her breath away.

Her arms wrapped around him, glorying in his superior physical strength as the hard muscles in his back moved beneath her palms. His skin was finely slicked with sweat, and his breathing was harsh and ragged against her ear—and with a sudden certainty she knew that even though it was only her body that interested him it was at least specifically *her* body that he had wanted; it wasn't just any body that would do.

That knowledge gave her a small glow of confidence. At least it was a beginning, a small seed that she could nurture with careful attention, by being as far as possible the perfect lover—challenging yet acquiescent, ensuring that she kept herself in prime condition for him, never refusing his demands. That way she could keep him wanting her—until, maybe one day, the wanting could grow into something more...

But right now she couldn't think any more. She was melting in a warm, honeyed tide of response, drowning in it, her body moving beneath his in a slow, languorous, erotic rhythm as the sweet aching rapture coiled inside her, her blood heating to a fever that was making her dizzy and delirious, until she heard her own voice sobbing in agonised need, and her body arched to meet the urgent thrust of his as he pounded into her, hard and fast.

The pure, primitive pleasure had taken hold of her, sweeping away any hint of restraint. This was no civilised lovemaking—this was a barbaric act of possession. But they were well-matched—her fingernails digging into his back as his teeth raked her smooth shoulder, their bodies locked together in the grip of a timeless, elemental force that was sweeping them both beyond the bounds of their mortal souls into a world of mindless ecstasy, their sanity lost, until at last, with a final shuddering convulsion, they both slipped over the edge to spin and fall through an endless of vortex of time and space—to collapse in a breathless, bemused heap on the rug in the quiet, elegant drawing-room as the last haunting notes of the saxophone died away.

CHAPTER NINE

MADDY woke to a perfunctory knock on the door, and before she properly had time to assimilate the fact that she was in Leo's room instead of her own her son—still in his tartan dressing-gown and dinosaur slippers—came bouncing in. "Uncle Leo, Uncle Leo—I didn't wake you up, did I?"

Leo groaned, pulling the covers up over Maddy's shoulder. "Yes, you did, you atrocious little monster," he responded with weary resignation. "What's so important that couldn't wait?"

Jamie was not at all perturbed by this ungracious welcome. "I just thought you would like to know that I scored five thousand one hundred and seventy two," he announced proudly, coming forward to display his computer game. "Oh, hi, Mum," he added cheerfully, climbing on to the bed. "I thought I was going to get knocked out at three thousand, but I managed to get out of it, and after that it seemed to just go and on."

"I'm delighted to hear it," Leo responded with a heavy irony that was totally lost on the seven-year old, who took him totally at face value.

"I thought you would be," he confided. "Now you can make an even more difficult one, and I'll see if I can get a big score on that."

"I shall start work on it at once."

"Will you?" Jamie bounced excitedly on the bed. "What are you going to call it? EcoWarrior 2?"

"That seems suitably creative," Leo responded drily.

It began to dawn on Jamie that he was being teased, and he returned his demi-god a look of reproach. "I was only making a suggestion," he protested. "You don't have to call it that if you don't want to."

Leo grinned at him and ruffled his soft brown hair. "Have you had breakfast yet, Half-pint?" he asked.

"No." Jamie looked a little guilty. "I was playing EcoWarrior in bed, before I got up."

"Well, why don't you go down to the kitchen and ask Auntie Peggy to fix you up with something?" he suggested.

Jamie nodded, relieved to have escaped without a scolding. He slid off the bed and scampered for the door.

"Oh, and Jamie," Leo added, with a note in his voice that warned that he was serious, "in future, would you mind knocking *before* you come into this room?"

Jamie looked slightly puzzled, but then enlightenment dawned on his small face. "Oh, yes—you'll be married, won't you?" he queried, only the faintest hint of disgust in his tone. "Do you have to knock on *every* door when there are married people?"

"No," Leo informed him solemnly. "Only the bedroom."

Jamie's brows furrowed again. "Why?" he wanted to know.

"I'll...explain that to you another time," Leo managed to respond, his body shaking with suppressed laughter. "Now, scarper!"

"OK!" Jamie flashed him a wide, ecstatic smile and darted out, closing the door behind him.

Leo rolled over, capturing Maddy beneath him before she could escape. He was still laughing, and she glared up at him indignantly.

"That wasn't funny!" she protested. "Why didn't you at least lock the door? What if he'd come in and found us..." Her voice trailed away—she couldn't quite bring herself actually to say the words.

"Making love?" he supplied teasingly. "You're right, of course—I wasn't expecting him to be up and around so early in the morning. I shall be more careful in future. Last night I...had other things on my mind." He ran a hand down over the soft curves of her body, savouring the silken texture of her skin, and back up to encompass the ripe fullness of one breast.

She tried to wriggle away from him, struggling to resist her own instinctive desire to surrender to what she knew he intended.

"Where are you going?" he growled.

"I'm...going to see Jamie," she insisted. "To... explain to him why I was in here."

"He knows why you were in here," he pointed out, refusing to let her go.

"I...have to go and see him." Her voice was rising on the edge of hysteria. "I have to see if he's all right. It could be psychologically damaging for a child of that age——"

"Don't be stupid," he argued impatiently. "He took it entirely as a matter of course—he's old enough to know that married people require a little privacy now and then."

"But we aren't married yet," she countered desperately as his thumb began to brush in treacherous caress over the taut, tender bud of her nipple.

"Not for another seven hours," he concurred, the husky timbre of his voice close to her ear. "But it was your idea to anticipate the ceremony. You can't change your mind now."

"Leo..." she protested, her resistance weakening beneath the sweet torment he was wreaking on both her aching breasts.

For answer he caught both her wrists, pinning them to the pillow above her head. "Any time, any place, any way I want," he reminded her, his strong thighs pushing between hers and forcing them wide apart. "That was the deal—and you're going to stick to it."

What could she do? As he thrust into her, hard and fierce, her body could only submit to his demanding possession, her spine arching as she moved with him, the inevitable response flooding through her in a warm, honeyed tide.

The thought passed fleetingly through her bemused brain that she really ought to be exhausted by now. They had made love all through the night—twice downstairs and several more times since he had carried her, naked and protesting, up here to his room—and had only finally fallen asleep a couple of hours ago.

And it had been incredible; nothing like Jeremy's enthusiastic but somewhat self-centred approach—Leo knew exactly how to touch and caress her to reduce her to a state of mindless ecstasy. And he seemed to enjoy doing it to her, watching her skin flush and her eyes mist over, making her breasts ripen and her nipples harden and her slender thighs part in wanton invitation, destroying any claim she might have had to being a reluctant participant.

And as he moved inside her, stretching her deliciously with each deep, driving thrust, she could hear her own breathing becoming harsh and ragged as the pleasure mounted, coiling inside her like a taut spring, and her body arched beneath him as she surrendered herself totally to his fierce demand—until at last the tension ex-

ploded, surging through her like molten gold, to leave
her weak and aching with satisfaction, crushed beneath
him on the bed.

The wedding took place in the church where she had
married Jeremy, but beyond that there was very little
similarity. There were only a few dozen guests, for one
thing, instead of the three hundred that had been invited
to the first, and she and Leo had greeted them at the
door, and gone in with them, avoiding the awkwardness
of that long walk down the aisle and the farce of being
"given away".

And her outfit was very different from the fairy-tale
crinoline she had worn then, with its frills and flounces
and silk flowers. It was a suit of smooth pale green
shantung silk, cut on very flattering lines like an Ed-
wardian lady's riding-dress, with a high collar and long
tight sleeves, which buttoned at the wrist, and nipped in
around her dainty waist above a deep peplum that flared
softly over the slender curve of her hips. And with it she
wore a rather dashing wide-brimmed hat, trimmed with
white and green silk roses.

Leo had accorded her a definite mark of approval
when she had first arrived at the church.
"Very...elegant," he had remarked, letting his eyes drift
down over her in a detailed appraisal that was unmistakably charged with sexual undertones. "Very elegant
indeed."

She had stood there, trying to hold her head up, as
that lingering gaze had made her all too conscious of
the way the softly tailored lines of the jacket moulded
the ripe swell of her breasts, the way the knee-length
skirt skimmed over her slender thighs. And her traitorous
body, remembering the night and his repeated pos-

session, had responded instinctively, so that her cheeks had flushed and her lips parted on a ragged indrawn breath.

He had laughed softly, one hand sliding down over the soft curve of her hips to pat her neat *derrière* in a casual assertion of seigneurial rights. "Later," he had taunted in a husky drawl. "We'd better get the formalities out of the way first."

And so she had had to stand there at his side, greeting their guests with a smile, and now she had to sit here with an outward semblance of composure as they waited for the last of the guests to settle in their pews and the vicar to start the service, while inside her emotions were churning. Her attempt to ease the tension by confronting it last night had backfired on her; she felt more apprehensive than ever.

The organist had been playing quietly in the background, but now, as the vicar came forward, the music ended, and a rustle of expectation whispered between the cool stone pillars that held up the lofty roof. Leo took Maddy's hand, and as if she had no independent will she rose obediently to her feet to stand beside him at the altar.

The day she had married Jeremy, when Leo had been best man, he had worn a morning suit—beautifully tailored across his wide shoulders, she recalled—and he had looked better in it than any of the other men present. Today he wore a more conventional suit, but the cut was as fine, and it did as little to disguise the impact of that raw masculinity.

And this was the man she was committing herself to, she reflected with a touch of panic... "With my body I thee worship..." The words came out as a husky whisper, and as she lifted her eyes reluctantly to his she knew that he was mentally undressing her, savouring the memory of holding her naked body in his arms, claiming already the rights that she was handing over to him so obligingly.

She drew in a deep, steadying breath, her aching breasts lifting beneath the smooth pale green silk of her jacket. She would have been grateful for the protection of a veil to hide behind, but at least everyone would assume the blush of pink that had risen to her cheeks was a becoming bridal modesty; she could only hope that none would guess it was due to thoughts wholly inappropriate to the solemnity of her surroundings.

The service seemed to be over so quickly that Maddy hardly had time to absorb that it was happening before she found herself once more in the small vestry where Leo had kissed her that very first time, so long ago. The guilt of that memory stabbed through her like a knife, and she stepped away from him quickly, before he could repeat the incident.

Fortunately the room quickly filled up with people, and with the fuss of signing the register she was able to avoid too much contact with him. In fact she was able to avoid it throughout the light wedding-breakfast that had been arranged back at the house, and even on the short journey by chauffeur-driven car to Manchester airport to catch their flight to Antigua for their honeymoon, innocently abetted by an eager Jamie, who had wanted to come along to see their plane taking off.

It wasn't until they were thirty-five thousand feet above the dark Atlantic, cocooned in the luxury of the first class cabin of a giant 747, that she really felt as if she was alone with him for the first time. The cabin was half-empty, the few other passengers asleep after a three-course dinner—served on fine bone china and accompanied by crisp champagne—that would have done justice to the finest restaurant.

They had flown westward into the setting sun, but now it was night, the sky here above the clouds a velvet black, swept by so many stars that it looked as if a casual hand had dropped a swathe of diamonds across it. Maddy sat gazing out of the small window at her side, lulled by the warmth of the softly lit cabin and the steady, quiet hum of the powerful engines on the wings beneath them.

Leo wasn't asleep either, although his eyes were closed; he was listening to a jazz concert on the headphones provided, his hand moving slightly as he absorbed the rhythms of the music. She glanced down at the plain band of new gold on the third finger of his left hand, matching her own. She was his wife now, the object of palpable envy from the smart stewardess who had served them their dinner. If only she had known the truth...!

As she sensed him stir as the concert ended she turned quickly to gaze out of the window again, her eyes not really seeing the silver stars—the reflection of the cabin was more real, of Leo leaning forward as he took off his headphones and stretched his arms above his head to loosen up his neck and shoulders.

"Not sleeping?" he enquired softly.

She was forced to turn back to him, though her eyes couldn't quite meet his. "No. I... don't find it very easy to sleep on planes. I expect I'll sleep like a log tonight."

He lifted one dark eyebrow in provocative enquiry. "You think I'll let you sleep?"

A hot blush sprang to her cheeks. "I... You can do what...you want to do first," she stammered awkwardly.

He laughed, harsh and mocking. "Oh, thank you. I can furkle around like a damned adolescent while you're dozing off in the middle of it, is that it? I'm sorry, but that wasn't what I had in mind.''

She drew in a long, steadying breath, bitter humiliation twisting inside her like a knife. ''I . . . didn't mean it like that,'' she responded in a choked voice. ''I'll keep my promise.''

''Any time, any place, any way I choose?''

She nodded, unable to speak.

He laughed softly. ''I'm not entirely convinced,'' he purred on an unmistakable hint of menace. ''Perhaps we should put it to the test.'' With a sudden movement he leaned across and unfastened her seat belt, and then, taking her wrist in a firm clasp, he dragged her ruthlessly to her feet.

She stared up at him in shocked realisation of his intention. ''What do you . . . ? No! We can't! Not here . . .''

''Oh, yes, we can,'' he asserted forcefully. ''Everyone else is asleep—unless you choose to make a scene and wake them up.''

For a brief moment she considered it, but she knew that he would simply find some other way to punish her, so with her heart thumping she let him hustle her back, past the other sleeping passengers, to the small washroom at the rear of the cabin.

It was as beautifully appointed as the rest of the first class accommodation, with a vase of freshly cut pink roses on the small vanity-shelf beneath the well lit mirror spilling their sweet fragrance into the air. But once they were both inside, with the door locked behind them, there was barely room to turn around.

''Leo, please,'' she protested desperately. ''This is crazy. Can't we go back to our seats? We'll be at our hotel in a couple of hours . . .''

"I want you *now*," he countered with fierce urgency, pushing her back against the vanity-shelf and starting to unfasten the buttons of her jacket. "You accepted my terms—any time, any place, any way. Well, this is what it means."

He didn't even bother to finish unfastening the buttons—he simply pulled the jacket down over her shoulders, dragging with it the straps of her white lace bra, effectively trapping her arms at her sides and leaving her breasts naked, their creamy swell tipped with tender nubs of pink that already were hardening in response to the heat of his dark gaze as it lingered there in possessive pleasure.

She drew in her breath, letting it go in a shuddering sigh. Yes, she had accepted his terms; but she hadn't known he had meant it so literally as this. She was to be no more than a plaything, for his exclusive gratification—and last night she had been stupid enough to hope that it could lead to something deeper. What a fool!

He smiled slowly, reaching out one hand to caress her ripe breast, and she caught her breath on a suppressed sob of pleasure as the pad of his thumb rolled over the taut peak, squeezing and tugging at it to arouse it to exquisite sensitivity. There was nowhere to escape from him; she was trapped, the hard edge of the vanity-shelf digging into her thighs as she leaned back against it.

"That's better," he murmured, satisfied at her compliance. "You have an exquisite body, you know—skin like silk and breasts like ripe peaches. And such delicate pink nipples...so inviting..."

He bent his head, his hot tongue rasping over one tautly aroused peak, his hard teeth nipping at it playfully, and she felt her spine slowly melting as the pleasure swamped through her. Already she had forgotten where

she was as with consummate skill his mouth and hands
made a feast of her aching breasts, wreaking havoc with
her senses.

But then, as his hands slid down to lift the hem of
her skirt up over her silk-clad thighs, cold reality returned with a thump. If she let him do this to her—and,
God forbid, let him force her to enjoy it—she would be
left with no self-respect at all. From somewhere she
found the strength to push him back, twisting away from
him.

"No..." she protested raggedly.

"No?" His smile was mocking, and with an abrupt
movement he caught her shoulders, turning her round
to face her own reflection in the brightly lit mirror. He
was arching her back against him, so that her breasts
were thrust proudly forward, softly blushing with the
same pink as the roses on the vanity-shelf, the nipples
a deep, ripe crimson, pert and inviting, still glistening
damp from the touch of his mouth.

"Look at yourself," he growled, his hot breath fanning
her bare shoulder. "Look at yourself and tell me you
aren't enjoying this."

She stared helplessly at the reflected image as his hands
slid round to cup the firm swell of her breasts, then
crushed them beneath his palms, circling over them, the
tender nipples scoured by that delicious abrasion. How
could she deny it? The evidence was there for him to
see.

He recognised her surrender with a sardonic smile of
satisfaction, and then once again his hands slid down to
lift the hem of her skirt, with slow deliberation drawing
it up over the slender length of her thighs, right up to
her waist, tucking it up beneath its own waistband.

Beneath it she wore only a dainty lace suspender belt and matching lace briefs, their pure whiteness a mockery of virginal innocence that seemed to offer an indecent invitation to his predatory lust.

"I like your taste in underwear," he taunted huskily. "Very sexy."

She gazed at the two people in the mirror; it was almost as if it was happening to someone else as his fingers slipped beneath that dainty scrap of white lace. But as she felt their touch intrude into the soft, secret velvet crease between her thighs a shiver of heat ran through her, like a fever in her blood, and she had to lean back against him for support, her eyes fluttering shut.

"Open your eyes," he commanded softly. "I want you to watch."

As if solely under the command of his will she obeyed, fascinated by the image of her own body responding so fluidly to the expert caress of his hands—one on her breast, the other dipping into that most intimate part of her. He had succeeded in reducing her to exactly what he wanted—merely a plaything, an object of his sexual pleasure, existing only to serve his remorseless demands. And, to her bitter shame, she knew that she liked it.

"That's better," he murmured. "You know we're going all the way, don't you?"

"Leo, please..." she protested, shaking her head weakly.

For answer he slid her tiny briefs down over her slender hips, letting them fall around her ankles. "Now, bend forward, and spread your legs apart," he ordered in that husky tone.

She hesitated, stubborn pride prompting her to resist, though she knew it was useless—he would take what he wanted, with or without her consent. And she had already effectively given her consent—not just by marrying him, but by marrying him when she knew what he wanted from her. She couldn't pretend that she had been under any illusions.

The warning glint in his eyes denied her final plea for mercy; he would brook no resistance from her. And so she leaned forward over the vanity-shelf, bracing herself with both hands on each side of the mirror, watching her own face, her lips parting slightly in shock as he took her with one deep, powerful thrust.

He was leaning over her, one hand supporting his weight against the wall, the other still caressing her breast, his hot mouth in the hollow of her shoulder where his languorous tongue was tracing tiny circles over the thudding pulse-point there, as they moved together in an erotic rhythm, locked in primitive passion.

Her breathing was ragged and harsh, her body flushed with pink, her eyes almost black and sparkling like jet as the sweet tide of pleasure surged through her. She was moving against him, totally receptive to that hard, driving possession as he thrust repeatedly into her, arching her back to crush her breast into his hand, wantonly submissive to all his demands.

The roaring of the aircraft engines had been reduced to the sound of her own blood roaring in her ears; her eyes were misted in the soft glow of light reflecting in the mirror. She was lost to all sense of shame at what she was doing, her self-respect sacrificed to a love that would obey his every command.

The sweet tension inside her was knotting in the pit of her stomach, its tentacles coiling through her limbs, drawing her nerve-fibres so tight that it seemed as though they would snap... Until with a final gasp and shudder it burst and unravelled, leaving her weak and helpless, collapsed against the cool hardness of the mirror as Leo took the last of his own satisfaction.

He laughed softly, mocking her dishevelled state as he drew her to her feet and turned her around. "That was very good," he approved tauntingly. "And I shall expect you to be as compliant as that every time. Now, you'd better tidy yourself up a little before you come back to your seat."

He let himself out, closing the door behind him, and she locked it before leaning back against the wall opposite the mirror, staring at her own reflection again. There was no point in pretending to herself—she had enjoyed it. It was the aftermath that was so bitter—knowing how little it had meant to him. It was all just part of his revenge.

A small piece of confetti fluttered from beneath the collar of her jacket. She picked it up, a bitter thought flitting through her brain. Don't wish too hard—your wish might come true. Well, her wish had come true—she was married to the man she had loved for years; she ought to be blissfully happy. But the price was very high—and she had only just begun to pay.

It should have been an idyllic honeymoon. They stayed on a tiny, privately-owned island, a short hop by sea-plane from Antigua. The only house was the villa in which they were staying—set in its own sumptuous tropical gardens, running down to a white, palm fringed beach—and the service was so discreet that they hardly saw the maid who came in and tidied up each day, re-filling the vases in every room with fresh orchids from the garden and ensuring that the fruit bowls were filled with ripe, succulent, colourful fruit.

But within hours of their arrival the battle-lines had been drawn for a bitter war of attrition. Maddy, exhausted from the flight and the effects of jet-lag, and from the weeks of strain and sleepless nights that had preceded the wedding, had gone straight to bed, collapsing into a deep, heavy sleep that did little to make her feel rested.

She woke with the sun streaming into the bungalow, to find Leo sitting on the bed beside her. "Good morning," he greeted her, a faintly sardonic smile curving that firm, finely-drawn mouth. "Do you feel better? You've slept around the clock."

Acutely conscious of the way the low-cut lacy bodice of her nightgown revealed rather too inviting a glimpse of the soft shadow between her breasts, she drew the covers up defensively, easing away from him. "Yes, thank you," she responded stiffly. "I slept very well."

He laughed, a low, husky laugh, and reached out to pull away the sheet she was clutching to her throat. "Why so shy?" he taunted. "I slept beside you in that rather fetching scrap of silk you have on—it's a little late now to be modest about it."

Angrily she resisted his attempts to pull the sheet away. "Leave me alone," she protested. "I want to get dressed."

"And *I* want you to get undressed," he countered, capturing both her wrists and jerking her towards him. "We had an agreement, remember? And you promised me faithfully that you would keep your side of it."

Her eyes spat sparks of fire at him as he forced her down on the bed, her wrists trapped above her head in one of his strong hands as he ruthlessly dragged the sheet away and surveyed the slender length of her body, inadequately concealed by the filmy covering of silk.

"You can have this easy, or you can make it tough on yourself," he warned her grimly. "I don't particularly care whether you enjoy it or not."

For answer she turned her set face away from him, refusing to give him the slightest sign of a response as he slid his hand down over her body, savouring through the filmy silk and lace of her nightgown the ripe swell of her breasts, the smooth curve of her stomach, the slender length of her thighs... He could take her body, but she would no longer allow him to take more than that; she had to bury herself somewhere deep inside, where he couldn't touch her, couldn't hurt her...

"Damn you!" Abruptly he let her go. "It's no fun making love to a sack of potatoes! Is that how you played it with Jerry? Turning cold on him at a moment's notice? Making him feel like a worm for even wanting to touch you?"

"If you hadn't done what you did on the plane..." she snapped at him.

"Oh, so that's it! What's wrong? You're upset that I didn't show you enough respect? Or that I showed you what you really are? You may look like an ice-maiden, but you have the soul of a true harlot, my dear. You enjoyed every moment of that encounter on the plane—and don't even waste your breath trying to deny it."

"I didn't... I..." But how could she deny the accusation, when the scarlet blaze of humiliation in her cheeks betrayed that he was right. Snatching up the sheet to cover herself, she turned away from him. "Go away," she bit out. "I'm not even going to speak to you."

He laughed without humour, but with a casual shrug of his wide shoulders he walked from the room. "Suit yourself," he tossed back at her. "But if you're intent on turning this marriage into a battleground, you'd better be prepared for the fact that you could be the one to get hurt.''

Maddy lay in the bed, her fist in her mouth to stifle her tears—she would not let him see the slightest sign of weakness. However much he tried to humiliate her, she would fight back. How could she go on loving a man who had so little regard for her, who had married her only out of some twisted desire to punish her?

They had been going to stay for the full week, but two days of the tense, hostile atmosphere was more than enough for both of them. When Leo suggested at breakfast on the third day that they might as well go home early, she was more than happy to agree.

He had made no further attempt to touch her—he had even had all his things moved from their room and had slept elsewhere. Which was what she had wanted, of course. Except that she had lain awake each night in the wide, comfortable bed, unable to stop herself thinking about the night before their wedding, when they had made love on the floor—when it had almost seemed as if that might be the pathway through which they could find reconciliation, when it had seemed that they might have built something deeper than the purely physical relationship that Leo had said he wanted.

Maybe she had chosen the wrong strategy after all? Maybe time—and the intimacy that came from love-making—could have convinced him that he was so wrong about her, but now she didn't know how to change tack. She was trapped by her own obstinacy into a pattern that was driving them irrevocably apart. And he had been right in saying that she would be the one to be hurt—it was slowly breaking her heart.

CHAPTER TEN

THEY arrived home late on Wednesday evening to find the house in a state of chaos—the electricians had come in to do the rewiring, and there was scaffolding along the side of the east wing where the pointing was being repaired. Maddy slanted a wry glance at the coils of electric wire stacked in the hall; she couldn't deny that Leo had kept his side of the bargain—she could hardly claim to have done the same thing.

He had rung to let Mrs Harris know that they were coming home early, claiming it was due to urgent business; she had offered to stay on to have dinner ready for them whenever they arrived but he had assured her that they would eat on the plane, so she had compromised with a cold chicken salad that she could leave out in the dining-room.

"I . . . think I'll go up and get changed before we eat," Maddy murmured, needing a little time on her own after the strain of the long flight home. "I'll only be about half an hour."

"Don't rush," Leo responded with little interest. "I need to check through my messages."

She hesitated, her hand on the banister-rail, watching as he turned indifferently away from her to pick up his post from the heavy antique walnut sideboard, his mind already switched into other channels. She had known it would be difficult, but she hadn't thought it would be like this . . .

Slowly she climbed the stairs, a feeling of bleak desolation descending around her heart. There didn't seem to be anything she could do or say. Maybe when Jamie got home—he seemed to be a link between them, at least...

An invigorating shower made her feel a little better, washing the last of the sharp white sand of the Caribbean from between her toes. If only it were that easy to wash away the memory of the past few disastrous days, she reflected wryly as she pulled on a clean, crisp cotton shirt and a denim skirt, and brushed back her thick wheat-blonde hair.

A glance at her watch told her that it was almost ten o'clock. She really wasn't hungry, but she ought at least to try to do justice to Mrs Harris's efforts. Besides, she had already lost too much weight—she was beginning to look haunted. Perhaps a touch of blusher on her cheeks might make her look a little better, she mused, sitting down at her dressing-table and regarding herself critically in the mirror—she rarely wore it, but tonight she needed all the help she could get.

With a deft touch she brushed a light stroke of the soft rose powder across her cheekbones. "What do you think, Sooty?" she enquired of Jamie's kitten, who had strolled into the room and was wrapping itself affectionately around her shins. "Is that an improvement?" The kitten blinked at her in mild indifference, and turned his attention to the urgent task of washing his own sleek black fur. Maddy laughed, shaking her head. "And here I am asking a cat for advice! I think I must be going very quietly round the bend."

A tap at the door brought her head round sharply. It could only be Leo. "Come...in," she called, a slight tremor in her voice. Her eyes slid instinctively towards the bed; was that why he had come...?

As usual he had taken off his jacket, and had his tie hanging loose around his unfastened shirt-collar, his cuffs rolled back over those strong brown wrists. And, as usual, her heart began to beat a little faster just at the sight of him.

"I'm sorry to disturb you," he said, his coolly distant tone disabusing her instantly of any apprehension that he might have had seduction on his mind.

"That's all right," she responded, trying to sound pleasant.

"I've had the final report from the accountant about the winding up of Jeremy's estate—these are the papers." He had a thick folder of them in his hand. "There's just one thing that isn't clear. There doesn't seem to be any record of his maintenance payments to you."

She smiled in wry amusement. "That's because he never made any," it gave her some satisfaction to explain.

Leo frowned sharply. "None? Ever?"

"No." She shook her head in emphasis. "I still had a little money from my parents' insurance, and then I had my party business. It wasn't much, but it was enough."

He sat down on the bed, regarding her in puzzled bemusement. "But... you were entitled to claim support from him. Why didn't you?"

"Because I didn't want it. I could manage without it. I preferred to be independent—not to let any of you have the slightest excuse for saying that I'd just looked on him as a meal-ticket." She couldn't keep the bitterness from her tone. "Not that it made any difference—you were determined to think the worst of me anyway."

Those dark eyes still regarded her with a hint of scepticism. "Why didn't you tell me any of this before?"

"You never asked," she pointed out with a touch of asperity. "You just assumed. Just as you assumed I wasn't serious about carrying on with the business here. And when you found out I was, you did everything you could to undermine it."

He looked genuinely startled at that. "I did not!" he protested. "I never had the slightest objection to you setting up your business—though I confess I didn't expect you to be quite so brilliant at it. In fact, if you want to continue with it I'd be delighted. It would be nice to share the place with people who wouldn't normally get a chance to see it."

She regarded him warily from beneath her lashes. "So who was putting people off after they'd booked?" she demanded, her voice laced with suspicion. "Who fixed it with the local magistrates to stop me getting a licence, and then made sure the alternative arrangements I'd made fell through?"

"Not me," he insisted. "I don't even know any local magistrates, except..." Light dawned, and he laughed without humour. "Except Julia's next-door neighbour. And Nigel plays golf with the area sales manager of the brewery."

"You're saying it was them who wrecked my plans?"

"I wouldn't lay odds against it," he confirmed drily. "Oh, it would have been Julia's scheme, but it wouldn't have been too difficult for her to bully Nigel into it."

Yes, that rang true, Maddy mused, but she still wasn't entirely convinced. "And what about the land sale?" she enquired. "Don't tell me you didn't know anything about that?"

"Yes, I knew." Those agate eyes were hard with anger. "So that *was* the reason you were so set on holding on to the house. I suspected it was that, right from the beginning—you had no other reason to be so attached to the place. Sass tried to tell me I was wrong—she said you knew nothing about it—"

"But... it was Saskia who told me about it," Maddy protested. "Weeks ago—before—"

"Before you agreed to marry me?"

"Yes, but..." Her voice faded away. How could she explain it to him anyway? He would never believe that however desperate she might have been to hold on to the house, she wouldn't—couldn't—have married him unless she was in love with him. She had refused even to let herself believe it, until the night before their wedding...

"Don't bother trying to explain," he grated tersely, rising to his feet. "I don't think I'd want to hear your reasons anyway. My only concern now is that in spite of the way we feel about each other we put on some semblance of a normal married life—for Jamie's sake. I don't mean we have to sleep together, but it might be more appropriate if you moved into the room next to mine. You may want to have it decorated first, of course—in fact there may be a number of other rooms that you'd like to redecorate. The money will be available."

As he strode from the room she sprang up from the dressing-table, reaching out for him in a last desperate effort to make him understand—she had no idea what she was going to say, but she knew she couldn't go on like this.

"Leo... Please, I—" A sudden shrill siren ripped through through the air, and Maddy caught her breath in shock. "Oh, my God—it's the smoke-alarm...!"

The other alarms had picked up the message, and their hellish screech battered her ears as it reverberated through the house. Forgetting everything, she darted past Leo and along the passage, desperately searching for signs of smoke or flames. Maybe it was just a false alarm after all...? But she could smell it now, and as she raced down the stairs she spotted a faint orange glow beneath the door of the breakfast-room.

"Maddy!" Leo tried to catch her arm, but she dragged herself away from him; it was still only a small fire—if she was quick enough, she could put it out.

"Get the fire brigade!"

The breakfast-room was filled with smoke; an arm-chair that stood in the corner was smouldering, a small lick of flame creeping up the frill of chintz around the bottom. Had one of the workmen left a careless ciga-rette-end? She didn't have time even to think about it— she just grabbed a cushion and started trying to beat it out. But it had got too much of a hold—the flames were starting to spread up the back of the seat, dangerously close to the curtains.

Maybe she could get the chair outside? She looked around wildly, trying to gauge how difficult it would be to drag it to the door. But it was big and heavy—by the time she had managed it... More flames were springing up, and she snatched up another cushion, choking as she beat frantically with both hands.

"Maddy, don't be crazy—leave it!" Leo grabbed her arm again, trying to drag her away. But she shook him off fiercely.

"I have to put it out—the whole house could go up!"

"The fire brigade are on their way—let them deal with it."

"It could be too late by then..." She shook him off forcefully, lunging with the cushions as the flames touched the curtains. The fabric was old, and caught quickly, going up with a whoosh in front of her eyes. She fell back, startled, as the hot fire belched across the ceiling above her head, rekindling the armchair to add to the conflagration and filling the room with black smoke.

"No...!" With a scream of helpless rage she dived at the other curtains, trying to drag them down before they too caught fire, but before she could do anything she found herself caught around the waist as Leo dragged her unceremoniously from the room, slamming the door shut behind them.

"Let me go!" she wailed, struggling and kicking out at him in desperation. "The house will burn down."

"And you're not going to be in it!" he vowed, cursing as she twisted violently in her efforts to escape, almost dropping her as he fell to his knees. The hall, too, was filling with black smoke now as the flames licked beneath the edge of the breakfast-room door, but he still had one arm around her, and simply dragged her bodily out of the front door.

They were barely out of the house when the windows of the breakfast-room exploded with the heat, and the fireball surged outwards and upwards, orange tongues leaping for the sky, blowing out the door into the hall behind them. It knocked them both off their feet, sending them sprawling across the gravel of the drive as Leo rolled on top of Maddy to protect her from the showering shards of glass. She heard herself scream.

As soon as it was safe he dragged her away from the house, crawling with her on to the grass, and they both sat there staring as the fire raged, spreading now to the rooms beside and above the breakfast-room, the wicked orange flames dancing like demons through the beautiful old house. It was her worst nightmare coming to life before her eyes; turning her face into the front of Leo's shirt, she burst into tears.

Without a word he scooped her up in his arms and carried her away, across the wide front lawn towards the gate. People were running towards them now, from the houses in the village, some of them in their night-clothes. They were staring up at the burning house, uttering soft cries of sympathy.

"Bring her into my sitting-room," she heard Mrs Harris say. "Poor thing—still, at least the both of you are safe. Fancy it happening like that, the very night you got back from your honeymoon...!"

Clanging sirens, blue flashing lights and a swirl of huge red engines heralded the arrival of the fire brigade, but Maddy didn't want to look; they were too late. Hadley Park—her home, her beautiful home—was going up in flames. Her fingers closed convulsively around the golden locket at her throat. She hadn't believed it could happen to her again.

Leo carried her into Mrs Harris's cosy living-room and settled her down gently on the sofa. Painful sobs were racking her body and he cradled her tenderly against his chest, stroking her hair, soothing her with gentle words. "That house really *does* mean a lot to you, doesn't it?" he murmured, and there was an odd note in his voice, if she had been in any state to notice it.

"I wanted it to be my home," she sobbed, her mind's eye torturing her with an imagined tour around every room, showing her all the precious little personal items, the family heirlooms she had cherished, the irreplaceable photographs—all gone. "I haven't had a home since I was twelve, when our house burned down. I had nothing left—not even my toys."

"I...didn't know your house had burned down."

She nodded, clinging to him. "I was in hospital when it happened. Both my parents were killed—it was the middle of the night, and the smoke... I always wanted a home—that was all I ever wanted. And I loved Hadley Park—right from the first time I saw it. It had such a...comfortable feeling about it, as if all the generations that had lived there were smiling at you."

He laughed softly. "Yes—I think I know what you mean."

"I wanted it for Jamie." The tears choked her for a moment. "I wanted him to have what I hadn't had—somewhere he really belonged, that would always be a base he could come back to wherever he went and whatever he did. But now it's going to be exactly the same for him as it was for me—he'll come home and find everything gone... I even forgot about his little kitten—it's still in there. He'll never forgive me..."

"The kitten'll be okay," he assured her gently. "It was probably gone out of the cat-flap long before we were. And—more important—he's still got you," he added, putting his hand beneath her chin and making her look up at him. "He might not have had, with you being so stupid as to try to put the damned flames out yourself!"

"I didn't want it to burn down. I just couldn't bear to lose everything all over again." He didn't seem to mind that she was soaking the front of his shirt. "It's like...having your heart torn out. I always felt as if I didn't have any roots. I had to go and live with my Aunt Helen, at school. Oh, she was nice to me, but...I had nowhere to go in the holidays, when everyone else went home—I didn't have anyone to send a postcard to when we went away on school trips. Sometimes I'd go home with one of the other girls—especially Saskia—just for a weekend or something. But I never really enjoyed it— it used to make me feel worse. It was as if I was on the outside, looking in—it wasn't until I met Jeremy that I felt as though I was...on the inside, as it were."

"So that's why you married him," he mused. "To feel as if you belonged somewhere."

She nodded, lifting her misted eyes to look up into his. "I know it was the wrong reason..."

He shook his head, his hand gently stroking her cheek. "There are a lot of worse reasons than that," he murmured, a wry smile twisting his mouth.

"I did love him," she asserted sadly. "Maybe not quite in the way I should have, but..."

"Don't talk about it now," he soothed as the door opened behind him and Mrs Harris came in, bearing a steaming cup of cocoa. "We'll talk tomorrow. You drink your cocoa, and then try to get some sleep..."

"Where are you going?" she demanded, clinging to his hand; it felt so strong and solid—warm resilient flesh over hard bone, that smattering of rough, dark curls across the back of his wrist. "Don't go."

"I was just going back to see what's happening," he assured her gently. "I won't be long."

"No." She knew she was making a mistake, letting him see how much she needed him, but she couldn't bear to let him go. "Please...stay here. Don't leave me by myself."

"You won't be by yourself—Mrs Harris is here." But he yielded to the pleading in her eyes and sat down beside her on the sofa, his strong arm protectively around her shoulders. "It's all right—I'm not going anywhere," he promised.

Mrs Harris had offered them her bed, but Leo had assured her that they would be perfectly all right on the sofa. Maddy didn't think she would sleep anyway, but she did, her head in his lap, his hand still gently stroking her hair. It was the first time they had been together like this, without that intrusive spark of sexual tension between them—just a quiet companionship that she could all too easily have got used to.

But when she woke up he was gone. She sat up on the sofa, brushing the hair back out of her eyes, a heavy weight of sadness in her heart. She felt grimy from the smoke, and her clothes were torn and filthy—and the sharp scent of burning still lingered in the air. A tear welled into the corner of her eyes and she brushed it away. The yellow glow of sunshine behind the curtains told her that it was a lovely morning, but it wasn't easy to remember to be grateful that they were all still alive— the house had been like a person, too, and now it was gone.

She was still sitting there, trying to summon up the will to move, when Mrs Harris bustled in.

"Ah, you're awake, dear. That's good—how are you feeling?"

Maddy managed a crooked smile. "Not too bad, I suppose. Where's Leo?"

"Over the road, with the man from the fire department—they're just having a look at the damage. He said you were to have some breakfast."

"I don't really want anything..."

"He said you'd say that," Mrs Harris returned briskly. "But he said you was to eat something—even if it was no more than a slice of toast."

For a moment her mouth thinned in angry rebellion—even when he wasn't here in person, he was laying down his orders! But he was right, she acknowledged wryly—she had to eat something before she could face up to what she was going to see when she went back through those wrought-iron gates.

"H-how bad is it over there?" she asked tentatively.

"I haven't seen it myself," Mrs Harris responded with a cheerful smile. "But they say it isn't too bad."

Maddy slanted her a doubtful look—that remark was probably meant to soothe her. Well, she would find out the worst in a little while—after she had eaten her breakfast. "I could do with a wash," she said.

"Of course. The bathroom is just at the top of the stairs. Mind your head as you go up—the beams are a bit low. And I'll find you something to put on for the time being—you're about the same size as my Sara."

"Thank you."

She did feel a little better once she had washed the grit and smoke out of her skin and hair, and thrown away her ruined clothes. She was just finishing her breakfast when a car drew up outside and Jamie piled out, followed by his teacher. She hurried to the front door to let them in.

"Hi, Mum!" he greeted her excitedly. "Miss Kenny brought me home early, 'cos of the fire. Were there fire engines? I *wish* I'd seen it! Can we go and look?"

The teacher smiled at Maddy over his head. "I thought I'd better bring him home early—they rang me last night at the campsite to tell me what had happened, and I didn't want him to be worrying. I had to tell him about it, though.''

''Yes—thank you for bringing him,'' Maddy responded gratefully. She had been gripping Jamie's shoulders a little too tightly, and he was wriggling in protest. ''Would you like to come in for a cup of tea?'' she offered.

Miss Kenny shook her head. ''No, thank you—I have to get straight back to camp. It's a good job we were still away, isn't it?''

''Yes, it is...'' At least they *were* all safe. She still had Jamie—and as for Leo... Well, she would work that out in due course. ''Well, I suppose we'd better go and see whether there's anything left standing over there,'' she suggested, forced by Jamie's presence to put on a brave face.

''Good luck,'' Miss Kenny wished her. ''I hope...it isn't too bad.''

Maddy nodded, and, taking Jamie's hand, led him across the road and through the wide gates. The house was still shielded by the trees. Letting go of her hand, he skipped ahead to where he could see—and stopped dead, staring. Her heart in her mouth, she hurried to catch him up.

The sun was shining, and close beside her a blackbird was trilling cheerfully. As she came out of the shelter of the trees she could scarcely believe her eyes. The roof was still intact; the bay windows of the breakfast-room itself and the room above it were broken and blackened, and it looked as if the main hall was in a mess, but that seemed to be the total extent of the damage. The rest of the house was untouched.

A fire-engine and a red car from the fire department stood on the drive, amid pools of water and uncoiled hoses, and a couple of firemen were wandering about tidying up.

"I...can't believe it," she breathed. "I thought...there'd be nothing left of it."

"Another five minutes and there wouldn't have been," one of the firemen responded cheerfully. "If it had got up into the roof, there wouldn't have been a thing we could have done. Got smoke-alarms in there, haven't you?"

She nodded.

"Very sensible—don't suppose you'd be standing here looking at it like this if you hadn't. Mind how you go inside, ma'am—just keep away from that room on the left there, and the one above it."

"Thank you..." As if in a dream, she walked up the steps and through the charred front door. The hall was blackened—the floor covered in wet ash, the old walnut sideboard damaged beyond repair—and through the gaping doorway she could see that the breakfast room was completely wrecked, but incredibly the fire had barely touched the stairs. Even the giant aspidistra that stood in the corner—though a little the worse for wear—had survived.

"Can I go and look for Sooty, Mummy?" Jamie pleaded.

"Yes—mind how you go," she warned him.

Satisfied, he hurried off to the kitchen while she wandered over to open the door of the drawing-room, amazed to see that apart from a little smoke- and water-damage just inside the door it was perfectly all right. She leaned against the jamb of the door, breathing slowly, warm tears of relief welling into her eyes.

The dining-room, too, was untouched—the meal they hadn't eaten still set out on the table. Brushing away the tears, she moved on to check the library—but just as she got to it she heard voices. Leo—and Saskia. Her heart gave a painful thud, and she moved forward quietly to peer through the crack in the door. Saskia had her arms wrapped around him.

"...absolutely horrified when I heard—I came over straight away to see if you were all right."

As Maddy watched guiltily from behind the door Leo gently removed himself from the embrace. "That's very kind of you," he responded in level tones.

"It's such a shame!" Saskia gushed on. "I could just cry to see it. I always felt as though this place was my second home—I used to play here so much when I was a child. Do you remember? Jerry and I were always playing hide-and-seek, or climbing the trees."

"I remember you coming over once or twice, when Nigel was going out with Julia, but you were a little past the age of climbing trees by then," he returned drily. "I wasn't aware that you and Jerry were particularly close friends before that."

Saskia pouted. "Well, I... We practically grew up together."

"You were the same age, but you hardly knew each other. Stop romanticising, Sass—I'm really not in the mood for it at the moment."

She wrapped her arms around him again. "Oh, I know—how selfish of me, going on like that! Poor you—it must be dreadful to see your lovely house in this state."

"It's a good deal better than it might have been, thanks to Maddy's obsession with smoke-alarms," he remarked, firmly disentangling himself a second time. "Did you know about her losing her home in a fire when she was twelve? You never told me that."

"You never asked," she countered petulantly.

"No, I didn't. But you volunteered a great deal of information about her—not much of it painting her in a very good light, as I recall. Knowing what I know now casts a rather different complexion on things."

Saskia paled, and then a hot flush of anger coloured her cheeks. "What do you mean?" she demanded. "She told you, didn't she? The spiteful cow—she promised she'd never tell you...!"

Leo frowned at her, puzzled. "Never tell me what? What are you talking about?"

At that point Maddy decided she ought to stop eavesdropping and make her presence known. "No, I didn't tell him," she asserted, stepping round the door. "And I never intended to."

"Tell me what?" Leo repeated, a sharp note in his voice. He looked from one to the other, those shrewd eyes reading the situation. "Something neither of you wanted me to know? Something...about Jeremy?"

"You *did* tell him!" Saskia accused her fiercely.

"I'm just guessing," Leo countered, a note of warning in his voice. "Something about you and Jeremy? Now, what could it be that you wouldn't want me to know? Were you having an affair with him?"

Right on cue, Saskia's blue eyes filled with tears, and she tried to throw herself into his arms. He held her off.

"When did it start?" he persisted. "Or rather, did it ever stop? I always knew the two of you had a thing going on at one time. Were you sleeping with him while you were engaged to me?"

"Well, so what if I was?" Saskia argued, her face contorted with spite. "You had the hots for *her* from the first moment you saw her!"

Leo moved across the room and slipped his arm around Maddy's shoulders. "I know—and it wasn't something I was particularly proud of, since I was engaged to you at the time. But I could no more have stopped myself falling in love with her than stop myself breathing.'' Those agate eyes smiled down into Maddy's startled grey ones. "Maybe if I'd followed my heart that night, instead of stopping to think of you, a lot of things might have been different."

"I knew it!" Saskia screeched. "Why *shouldn't* I have had an affair with Jeremy, when she was the one who stole you from me?"

He shook his head. "No—you're wrong, Sass," he stated in a firm, quiet voice. "Maddy never did anything to come between you and me—not intentionally, at least. It wasn't her fault that I fell in love with her—she never gave me any encouragement. No, you were the one who spoiled whatever we might have had—you seemed such a sweet kid, but from the minute I asked you to marry me you changed. All you could think about was having the biggest diamond in your engagement ring, the most lavish wedding you could devise. I began to feel as if I was no more than a cheque-book to you. But, even so, I always felt guilty about the way I broke things off—always felt in some way responsible for you. But no more—you don't deserve it."

Saskia began to sob loudly. "It isn't fair!" she threw at Maddy accusingly. "I always used to be nice to you, even though you were the poor little church-mouse and never had any nice clothes. And it wasn't easy sometimes—you couldn't do *anything* for me! And now this is how you pay me back! I wish your stupid house had burnt to the ground!" And she ran from the room, slamming the door with a reverberating vigour somewhat at odds with her usual delicate mien.

Left alone with Leo, Maddy couldn't quite bring herself to risk lifting her eyes to his face; she kept them lowered, concentrating instead on the top button of his shirt. "Did you...mean that?" she whispered shyly.

"About falling in love with you?" he queried, a soft lilt in his voice as he drew her firmly into his arms. "Yes, I did. From the moment I saw you walking down those stairs, looking like a princess—even though your dress had seen better days. I was twenty-seven years old, with as much history behind me as any man of that age—I thought I was beyond that kind of reaction. In fact, I'd just made up my mind to do what everyone had been expecting of me for about as long as I could remember and marry Saskia."

"I felt the same," she confessed, a soft blush of pink creeping into her cheeks. "But I felt so guilty—she'd always been my best friend..."

"If I'd stayed—if I'd spoken to you..." he murmured, his warm breath fanning her hair. "But I needed time to think—time to work out if it could possibly be real, and to decide how to break it off gently with Saskia. So I made an excuse to go back to America for a couple of weeks. And then I had a letter from Jeremy, asking me to come home and be his best man!"

"I...had no idea how you felt," she breathed, gazing up at him. "I thought you were in love with Sass—that I would never have stood a chance. And Jeremy was so...lively, so charming—I thought I could make myself fall in love with him. I did try—and I don't think he ever guessed how I really felt..."

"He never guessed about you, though I think he did about me," he mused wryly. "I've sometimes wondered if that was part of the reason why he was in such a hurry to marry you—he had always tried to compete with me, right from when he was a kid, but he'd never quite been able to succeed. But with you, for the first time he was the winner—you were the one thing I really wanted, and he had you.''

Maddy sighed, leaning her cheek against his wide chest, contentedly breathing in the warm, musky scent of his skin. "If only I'd known. I thought you despised me. You hardly ever came home when I was there."

"I had to stay away. I felt like just about the lowest form of life, wanting you so much when you were married to Jerry... It made it a little more bearable if I could off-load some of that guilt on to you, by believing the very worst of you—with a little sly help from Saskia, it now appears. Of course, I should have seen through her—I should have guessed that something was going on between her and Jerry... But I felt so bad about breaking off our engagement that I would never let myself listen to my own suspicions."

Maddy nodded sadly, understanding. "But... didn't Jeremy ever talk about me?" she asked, a wistful note in her voice.

He laughed drily. "He'd have talked about you all the time if I'd let him. But I tried to avoid discussing you with him as much as possible—I was afraid he'd see how jealous I was. And anything he did say I just dismissed as being because he was so crazy about you. Which meant that Saskia was my only source of information about you—and I let her talk. I wanted to hear about you, even if it was all bad."

"But... you don't believe the things she said any more?" she asked tremulously. "You don't think I married you just to keep the house, and the money from the land?"

He stroked his hand down her cheek, smiling. "Not just for the money, no—but I do think perhaps your reasons were a bit tied up with the house. But I can understand that now—I understand how important it is to you. To have lost your home—everything—when you were so young must have been devastating for you. But this is your home now—you'll never have to feel as if you're on the outside again."

And, to prove his point, his head bent over hers, and their mouths melted sweetly together. It was just the kind of tender, loving kiss she had been aching for; held in the strong, protective circle of his arms, she felt that at last she had truly come home. His lips were warm and enticing, gently coaxing hers apart to admit the languorous swirl of his tongue as the familiar musky scent of his skin drugged her mind, soothing away all the painful memories. The tension was still there, but it was no longer the dangerous clash of bitter opposition—rather a strong, sustained, elemental force-field of matched desire. And as his hand slid slowly down her spine she felt herself melting against him, the need awakening inside her...

"I found Sooty." The door had burst open, and Jamie bounced into the room, hugging his little black kitten. "He was outside the back door—he was too scared to come in. But I gave him a saucer of milk, and he's all right now."

"James," Leo began, a distinct note of constraint in his voice, "what did I tell you about knocking on doors?"

"Yes, but you said only the bedroom," Jamie argued reasonably. "What were you doing?"

Maddy had to fight back an urge to giggle as Leo sought for a suitable response. "I was just kissing your mother."

"Ughh!" The small face puckered into an expression of total disgust. "Do you *have* to do that if you're married?"

"It...helps," Leo managed, his body shaking with suppressed mirth.

"Well, *I'm* never getting married, then," Jamie announced decisively. "I *hate* kissing girls!"

And he scooted off, leaving Leo and Maddy to collapse with helpless laughter. "Little demon!" Leo declared. "He asks the most awkward questions."

"Kids do," Maddy responded sagely. "You should have seen your face! You thought you were going to have to start explaining to him about the birds and the bees, didn't you?"

"I guess I'll have to pretty soon anyway," he remarked, drawing her back into his arms. "I was thinking maybe we might start considering a little brother or sister for him some time soon."

She stared up at him, puzzled. "But I thought...you didn't want children?"

He lifted one dark eyebrow in frank surprise. "What on earth gave you that idea?"

"Saskia said—"

As one, they shook their heads, wryly dismissing whatever Saskia might have said.

"I want children," he asserted. "Lots of them. What do you think?"

"I think...it's an excellent idea," she conceded, her eyes dancing merrily as they gazed up into his. "Though, as for Jamie, I think it's quite likely he'll still prefer his computer game!"

HARLEQUIN PRESENTS®

Dreaming of a white Christmas?

Lisa was—and Oliver Davenport made every one
of her Yuletide fantasies come true....

Share the most magical Christmas of all with Lisa
in

#1851 *HER CHRISTMAS FANTASY*
by
Penny Jordan

Harlequin Presents—the best has just gotten better!
Available in December wherever
Harlequin books are sold.

TAUTH15

by
Miranda Lee

Complete stories of love down under that
you'll treasure forever.

Watch for:

#1855 *A WEEKEND TO REMEMBER*

It was only a little white lie...but before she knew it,
Hannah had pretended she was Jack Marshall's fiancée.
How long would it be before Jack regained his memory?

Available in December wherever
Harlequin books are sold.

Look us up on-line at: http://www.romance.net

HARLEQUIN PRESENTS®

ATR1